Incident at Greasewood Junction

Yellowhenry and the Rattlesnake Venture

This book is a work of fiction

Chapter 1

Charlie Goodwoman was presenting his snakes as a demonstration project. They were all rattlers he had tamed till he could hold them in his bare hands, let them crawl his arms and neck, and poise by his face as they rattled loosely and flicked their tongues while staring at the mesmerized seventh grade kids who were shrinking down and back in their desks as Goodwoman grinned and moved closer to them. "These snakes told me that today is a day of no biting," he said.

A bit frightening in his own right, Charlie was a Native American of indeterminate age. He thought he was around sixty, but he hadn't aged well. His red face was leathery and deeply seamed, his eyes were deep set slits that glittered black, and his nose was blunted and bent off to the left a little. His smile revealed an even set of startlingly white teeth with very pronounced upper fang-like canines. At five feet eight inches in height and a hundred forty pounds he had adopted wide black elastic suspenders to keep his Levi's on his hips. He wore knee high snake boots and a black satin stovepipe hat. The hat sported a snakeskin hatband into which he had thrust three dyed chicken feathers. Red, white, and blue.

Suddenly the largest of the three snakes in his hands lost its purchase on his left arm and dropped to the floor where it slithered quickly toward an aisle between two rows of kids. Pandemonium ensued as the kids up front screamed and leaped wildly, their desks shoved and sliding at the snake that raised itself onto the seat of the desk that struck it. It began rattling loudly and lifted its upper body into a striking position. Goodwoman reached smoothly and snatched the big rattler by the back of the head with his left hand while carefully lifting its body with his right. He stepped away from the frantic kids and laughed as they raced to the classroom door, piling up in a panicked, screaming and terrified stack, scrambling and kicking over one another as they fell into the hallway where they ran for cover.

"Put those goddamned snakes back in their boxes!" Mr. Peacock, the seventh grade teacher shouted. Goodwoman, who had calmed the wildly rattling five footer, laughed in delight at the chaos of kids pummeling other kids in their horror and fear filled panic.

"Look," Goodwoman said. "Bo is as calm as any service dog."

It was true that the snake crawling behind his handler's neck was apparently soothed and no longer rattling or showing any interest in biting anything. "Just put 'em away," Peacock shuddered. "Put 'em away."

Goodwoman cackled, apparently delighted with the chaos his snakes had caused, "You got it, Coach," he said. "These are my kittens. They sleep with me at night. They are my no-biters." He tucked all three of his pets into his carry boxes.

"You mean you've defanged them, right?" Peacock asked hopefully.

"No, no. They couldn't eat without their teeth."

"How did you teach them not to bite you?"

"Time. After three years, or so, of constant strikes, they just give up. Then, as long as they're well fed, I can handle them like a garter snake."

"What if I tried it?"

Goodwoman cackled again, "You don't have my smell. But you can try it. Reach right in and pull one out."

Peacock leaned over one of the boxes and peered in at the big diamondback who looked at him through the glass covering. A sudden bang against the cover caused him to jerk back, nearly falling. "I guess you don't look right either," Goodwoman laughed delightedly.

"Mr. Goodwoman," Peacock said sternly, "please take your snakes and leave."

"Not without my hundred dollars," he said.

"Under the circumstances, there was no scientific value in what you presented."

"Okay, see if there is scientific value in antivenin," Charlie shouted, opening one of the boxes and reaching inside to remove a three footer. "Here, catch!"

The teacher threw his arms up defensively, jerking spasmodically as the thrown snake flopped over his arm and buried its fangs into his right forearm. "I'm bit, I'm bit!" Peacock screamed, throwing the snake, and running for the door where he stepped on the fingers of a girl who was just coming to from being dazed by the stampede that stormed over her earlier. She howled in pain and looked at Goodwoman, the only person left in the room who was shoving desks around apparently trying to find something.

She was just getting to her feet when the snake shot from under a desk and headed for the open door. The girl shrieked and started stamping her feet as she ran in place. The snake snapped into a quick coil and struck her in the right ankle, its fangs hanging up in her stocking as it tried recoiling, causing it to bite her again. She jerked her leg free and screamed in hair raising decibels that brought teachers running from both directions.

The snake made its way into the hall where it took up a defensive position by the wall away from the runners who suddenly veered away from it, shouting, "Snake! Snake!"

"It's okay, it's okay," Charlie hollered. "I've got him." He moved to pick up the snake, but it took a swipe at him. "Damn you, Petey," he yelled. He moved with a sudden fluid draw that produced a knife with a ten inch blade from his boot. "Bite this you ungrateful little bastard." He darted the blade edge toward the rattler that was buzzing its loudest as it reared into a striking pose. Its strike was aimed at his hand but he dropped the target and the bite hit the blade, fangs forward. The snake's head was neatly split between the venom sacks. The diamondback began twisting in a writhing spin. Charlie left it where it was.

He looked at the queue of teachers peering around one another. "Don't pick him up barehanded," he grinned. "That girl back there in the room ain't screamin' cause she's scared. She's been bit a couple of times. Peacock took the first bite. They both need to go get antivenin."

The teachers looked at him in stunned silence. "Hey," he shouted. "You got two people snake bit here. Chop, chop. Move, people."

One of the men teachers turned and moved around the twisting serpent and hustled to the classroom where he scooped up the screaming girl and ran back down the hall to the school offices. The rest of the teachers retreated, staring in shocked but mesmerized attention at the writhing serpent with its incessant buzzing that gave them the chills.

Captain Joe Yellowhenry was walking down the sidewalk toward his Montana Highway Patrol offices when he was passed by an ambulance that headed toward the community school complex. "What the hell?" he said to himself. When he walked into the patrol office, he asked the officer on the desk if he'd heard what was going on at the school.

"Snakebite's what came over the radio from the ambulance."

"Goddamnit, those fools let Charlie Goodwoman come in again to show his snakes to the kids. I told them last year to knock it off. That it would just be a matter of time until someone got bit."

"City Chief MacTavish has dispatched a unit to investigate."

"That's good. Do you know who?"

"Roland Hainlign."

"That's good. Roland is a good man. I'm going to drive over there and see what happened. See if I can give him a hand."

The scene at the school was one of shock and disbelief. Hainlign had taken a verbal report and was cautiously moving around something in the hall that was bloody and twisting and turning in and over itself as it buzzed furiously. "What you got there, Roland?" Yellowhenry called as he walked quickly past the wide double doored entry to the school offices.

"Rattler. Something wrong with it though," Hainlign replied glancing over his shoulder.

Yellowhenry approached cautiously. "Damned thing's head is split in two, isn't it?" he asked.

"Yeah, Joe, but it still strikes," Hainlign said nervously.

"Where's Charlie Goodwoman?"

"Haven't seen him. I guess he left out the back."

The school principal, Robert Goldman, a stuffy sixty year old, overweight and bald man of medium height saw Yellowhenry approach. "Good," he said loudly, "an Indian. Catch that damned thing and get it out of here before it bites someone else."

"I told you last year, Goldman, not to bring that act back. As far as I'm concerned, it ought to bite you," Yellowhenry retorted.

"What makes you think you know anything. Are you a herpetologist?" Goldman demanded.

"Aw, just shut up, you damned fool. Roland, we need to anchor it before it quits coiling and takes off. Hang here for a second. I'll be right back," Yellowhenry said. He hustled back to the school office and looked around. In a corner he spotted a rubber twenty-five gallon garbage can that was set up for recycling soda cans. He grabbed it and dumped the contents, about half the can, out on the floor. Then he ran back to where Hainlign was kicking at the snake that had stopped its paroxysms of coiling and recoiling. It was crawling down the hall away from the office.

Goldman, terrified, had taken off running. Hainlign's kicks made the snake stop. It was reared back in its striking pose with its split skull drooping off to both sides as it continued rattling. Yellowhenry approached with the can turned upside down. He slapped it down over the snake and pressed it firmly in place as the rattler struck against the sides. "Roland, see if you can locate the custodian. Tell him we need a shovel."

"Scoop shovel?"

"No. A garden spade. We can whack the snake and then chop its head off."

"Got it, Joe. I'll be right back."

Chapter 2

Outrage was the order of the day following the mayhem at the junior high school. The teacher who was bitten was blamed for the stupidity of allowing Goodwoman anywhere near the students with his damnable collection of snakes, even though he was licensed to possess them. Peacock blamed the principal for the continuation of the program that had allowed Goodwoman to present the snakes as he had for the previous four years. "I was just following the established program," he claimed.

When Goodwoman was questioned, he said, "That cheap bastard refused to pay me the hundred dollars for bringing my snakes to school. That ain't right."

The Hill County Sheriff, Lloyd Hickam, arrested Goodwoman for endangerment when it was discovered that he had tossed a fully envenomated rattlesnake at Peacock. Peacock acquired an attorney who sued Goodwoman for medical expenses and civil damages and the school for defamation when the principal and school board blamed him for endangering his students. Goodwoman sued the sheriff's department for wrongful arrest. The seventh grade girl's parents sued the school and Peacock for endangerment and medical expenses. A group of fifteen parents of students, who had suffered bumps, bruises and trauma, sued Goodwoman, Peacock, and the school district in a class action lawsuit claiming safety violations and negligence. When it became known that Yellowhenry had warned the school principal the previous year that it was just a matter of time till someone would be bitten by one of Goodwoman's snakes, the school board sued Yellowhenry for offering inexpert advice.

When Goodwoman was in jail, no one was taking care of his snake milking operation at his shack in Greasewood Junction fifteen miles west toward Shelby and three miles south of the Highline Highway. His incessant hollering at the deputies on duty finally irritated Hickam enough to call Yellowhenry. "Hey, Joe," he asked, "is there some way you could take Charlie out to his place so he can tend to his goddamned snakes. He has a lawsuit filed against us, so our hands are tied. We can release him into your custody."

"How long has he been locked up, Lloyd?" Yellowhenry asked.

"Four days."

"So, his snakes have had no one tending to them at all? Why didn't he post bond?"

"I guess no one but him tends the snakes. He claimed he wasn't going to pay a dime for bail because he wasn't at fault. He's been raising hell about it and he's going to add it to his lawsuit against us for wrongful arrest."

"Well, he has a legitimate business selling snake venom, Lloyd. So, for business interruption, he may have a point."

"That's what I'm conceding, Joe. If you could give me a hand, I'd sure as hell owe you one."

"Forget that, Lloyd," Yellowhenry said irritably. "But yeah, sure. I'll be over in fifteen minutes and pick him up."

When Yellowhenry and Goodwoman pulled into the dirt yard in front of Charlie's shack, Goodwoman began yelling, "Stop! You're gonna run over a snake."

"Where?" Yellowhenry said, slamming on his brakes.

"Back up. He's under your car."

The big five footer, nearly perfectly camouflaged, had coiled up in a defensive position. Yellowhenry watched as Goodwoman cautiously approached. The snake watched the man and began raising itself into a striking position while rattling loudly. "Oh, son of a bitch," he wailed. "This is Bo. He's my headliner. Now, he wants to bite. Three years of work gone in four damned days."

"Yeah, that's really the shits, Charlie," Yellowhenry observed. "Do you want me to shoot him for you?"

"No, don't do that. He's a good milker. I just have to secure him and put him back in his box."

"How the hell did he get out of his box?"

"The boxes just have pressure lids. No latches. He got hungry and went foraging. You can't blame him for that. He ain't been fed in over a week, thanks to law enforcement."

"So, what's going to keep him in his box if there's no latch?"

"We'll have to weight it down."

Suddenly the snake launched a strike that was a blur and would have scored on anyone but a snake handler. As it was, the fangs brushed the heel of Goodwoman's hand which he expertly offered and withdrew by lifting his elbow. He began circling and drawing strikes until he positioned the snake into a strike that exposed the rattles. He seized the big rattler by its rattling tail and jerked it up to full length, holding it straight out with his right arm. It dangled and twisted, but its strikes only covered half its body length. Then Charlie lowered it to the ground, giving it a few inches of crawling slack. He smoothly grabbed it behind the head with his left hand. Then he wrapped it around his left arm, handling it gently but maintaining his grip behind its head.

"He's okay, now, Trooper Joe," Charlie grinned happily. "By this time next year, he'll be good as new."

Yellowhenry stared at the lunatic as his hair crawled up the back of his neck. "Yeah, right, Charlie," he said from where he sat in his police cruiser. "So, that's one. How many snakes do you have?"

"It varies. I never know how many wild ones there are."

"Wild ones? What the hell do you mean, wild ones?"

"I have to raise mice for my milkers. The mice get away sometimes, so the wild ones come huntin'."

"Jesus, Charlie. I'm no snake handler," Yellowhenry said. "What the hell can I do, here? How many milkers do you have?"

"Fifteen. But they are my pets. I'll take care of the capture and reboxing. I can use your help feeding and watering them, though. You aren't afraid of handling mice, are you? I'll give you a pair of gloves."

"I can handle mice, but what about the wild ones. Where are they gonna be?" Yellowhenry asked nervously.

"Well, what size foot do you have?"

"Nine."

"Good. I wear a ten. Let's trade boots. Mine are snake proofs."

"You mean you get bit?"

"Oh, yeah. All the time. I don't kill any of the wild rattlesnakes, and I don't have time to keep moving them. I just tap them back out of the way."

"Okay, I guess," Yellowhenry said reluctantly. "I have to take you back to jail, so I'll give you a hand, but get rid of that snake on your arm and come back. I'm not getting out until I have your boots on."

Trooper Joe, as he was well known, watched Goodwoman cautiously open the door to his ramshackle home and suddenly step back. The man came hustling back to the car still carrying his big rattler. "Joe, is your trunk secure?"

"What do you mean?"

"I need to put Bo in a safe place. Your trunk, I hope."

"Why didn't you put him in his box?"

"Bull snakes. I counted four. They're killing my rattlers. You can shoot every bull snake in there. Hurry, pop your trunk lid. Bo will keep in there until I can get back to him."

"All right, there you go," Yellowhenry said, releasing the latch. "Hurry up and bring those boots back here."

Chapter 3

With their boots exchanged, Yellowhenry followed Goodwoman with his service revolver drawn. The inside of the place was a one room affair, with a sheep herder's stove in a corner near a single wide military cot with a sleeping bag draped off the side. A rattle snake was coiled up in the middle of the bag, hiding its head under its coils from the poised stance of a big bull snake that held its head frozen in place as it repositioned its body apparently trying to get the rattler to take a shot so it could be seized.

The rest of the room was set up with glass terrarium snake boxes set on folding tables along one wall. All were empty. The opposite wall was set up with a counter that featured drawers below and a milking station above. White mice were swarming the counter. Two small diamonbacks were crawling swiftly along the walls pursued by five and six foot bull snakes. One big bull was swallowing a rattler in the middle of the floor. "Shoot that bull snake on my sleeping bag!" Charlie screamed. "That's Felicia he's after. She's pregnant."

Yellowhenry pulled his Colt .45 into a two handed grip and squeezed off a round that obliterated the head of the big bull snake. Goodwoman darted to the coiled rattler, checked it for hostility, and, detecting none, carefully lifted it and carried it across the room, side stepping snakes, to a terrarium where he lifted the lid and gently set the snake inside. He replaced the lid and placed a rock from where it lay next to the snake box onto the lid.

Yellowhenry began stalking the remaining bull snakes. He left the one alone in the middle of the room and after kicking aside a pair of snakes that banged his boots, he quickly shot the other two bull snakes. Goodwoman cackled, "Hell, Joe. You could have let those two live. They were chasing wild ones."

"Really," Yellowhenry returned as he blew away one of the rattlers, coiled and rattling insanely.

"Hey, they'll crawl out after a bit. You don't have to shoot 'em," Goodwoman shouted.

"Oh, yeah," Yellowhenry said as he blew the head off the big bull snake swallowing the rattler in the middle of the room. "I'm just gettin' warmed up."

"Well, I will say I'm glad you took out that big bastard, Joe," Charlie said grimly. "He was eatin' Gladys, another one of my pregnant females."

Yellowhenry stalked to where the second wild prey snake had coiled up, adding its intense rattling to the scene of snakes that were suddenly alarmed at the activity of the two men and were coiling and rearing into the 'S' shape of the breed when a strike was imminent. All of them were rattling madly. His shot ripped the snake, that had suddenly struck, nearly in two about a foot from the tail of its four foot length. It began striking wildly.

"That's just cruel," Goodwoman shouted. "That's like if I gut shot you. How'd you like that?"

"It might be better than the nightmares I'm gonna have after this," Yellowhenry gritted. "You can be merciful to that damned thing. I don't care. How many more snakes do you have left to corral?"

"Eight, but they are all milkers, so don't shoot no more."

"All right. I'm gettin' out of here. Call me when it's time to feed the snakes."

Twenty minutes later, Goodwoman came walking out to where Yellowhenry was leaning against the front of his car. "I just have to get Bo out of your trunk, Joe. I want to thank you for giving me a hand."

"That's all right, Charlie. All in a day's work. I'll pop the trunk lid for you."

The big rattler was gone. "He ain't here, Joe," Goodwoman announced.

"Did he get out?" Yellowhenry asked, alarmed.

"I don't think so. He's somewhere in your car."

"Oh, for Chrissakes, Charlie. We can't have that. You've got to find him."

The men searched for half an hour, tearing the back rest of the back seat loose and looking under the seat. They were unsuccessful, but they finally heard it rattle on the passenger side of the car somewhere down where they couldn't get at it.

"Charlie, we're forced to leave Bo there," Yellowhenry finally announced. "Let's go take care of the rest of your snakes. Maybe he'll crawl back into the trunk or the backseat if we leave him alone for awhile."

Back inside the shack, the men split the work with Yellowhenry capturing mice with a fly fisherman's close-meshed net. He grabbed them by the tail and whacked their heads on the edge of the counter and tossed them to Goodwoman who placed them inside the boxes with the snakes. While he waited for a mouse, Charlie added clean water to pans that were placed in each box. It took most of an hour to finally complete the work. There were still white mice running loose when they were finished. "Just let 'em go, Joe," Charlie instructed. "The wild ones will come back and slick 'em up."

"I thought I killed the wild ones. You can't keep the mice in the drawers, huh?"

"You have no idea the number of wild ones around here," Goodwoman laughed. "When I'm here, I keep the mice fed and watered so they stay put. All they do is lay in the sawdust, feed, get fat, and reproduce. When they're neglected, like now, they chew their way out and roam around. That's part of my lawsuit against the county."

"Jesus, Charlie. You have a nice operation here. I'm going to see if I can get you released on your own recognizance. I'll bring you back if we can get that handled. You need to be here every day."

"That's for damned sure, Joe. This place doesn't take care of itself."

Bo, the rattler, did not crawl back to where he could be retrieved. Yellowhenry did manage to get Goodwoman released on his own recognizance, but Charlie drove back in his own rig. Yellowhenry followed him in the hope that Goodwoman's favorite snake would reverse itself and crawl back into the trunk. It didn't. He was forced to drive off with the big snake holed up in the framework of his cruiser.

It rattled from time to time as it starved to death. Yellowhenry had dumped the cruiser in the shop where the mechanics refused to make any attempt to release the big snake and Yellowhenry refused to drive the car despite its having been custom painted for him. What the mechanics feared was that the snake would attack as soon as it was released, or find its way out and be found loose somewhere in the shop. Every morning one of them pounded on the rocker panels on the passenger side of the car while another listened with a stethoscope. The snake moved around from front to back and rattled in response to the pounding, but it stayed put. It was finally removed when it died and began to smell as it decayed.

Yellowhenry finally got his car back six weeks later. He became accustomed to the faint odor that clung to the inside, but prisoners he transported, bitched about the smell of something dead. He smiled and explained that a big rattler was trapped under the rocker panels. "He's probably dead by now, but call out if he comes up from under the seat," he warned seriously. "Damned thing's near seven foot long."

Chapter 4

An upshot of Yellowhenry's assisting Charlie Goodwoman was the latter's sudden declaration of undieing friendship for the young highway patol captain. Goodwoman came to town about twice a month for supplies and an overnight visit. He drove an old 1954 Dodge pickup that he parked next to the fire hydrant up the street from the patrol office. He was ticketed every time, but he ignored the summons.

He began his visit at the patrol office where Yellowhenry gave him a half hour to explain how things were going at his snake ranch, and ended at Minnie Grave's home where the man spent time chasing the woman around until she retreated to Yellowhenry's house next door.

Minnie, Yellowhenry's next door neighbor, was a widowed Cree who had adopted Yellowhenry, his wife, Amy, and their half dozen children, whom she grandmothered. She was a white haired sprite who declared Yellowhenry's horse, a sorrel gelding called Hi Boy, as 'our' horse. They shared an oversized septic tank and drain field which allowed both neighbors to enjoy indoor plumbing, a very nice improvement to their reservation homes. Amy teased Minnie, who loved teasing others, that if she'd just give in and let Goodwoman have his way, she'd be able to marry him and move out to his snake ranch at Greasewood Junction.

"I like the idea of having a man, but that one has those teeth that make me feel like he'd be going for my neck every time he mounted me," she shuddered.

"Maybe Joe can make him a muzzle," Amy giggled. "Then all he could do is growl."

"I'm afraid he'd rattle," Minnie laughed. "No. I'll feed him, let him shower up, while I wash his pants and shirt, but that's it. I don't care if he does chase me around the house, naked and floppin' while he waits for his clothes to dry. I ain't takin' him on."

"Do you want me to talk to him, Minnie?" Yellowhenry asked.

"If he catches me, maybe. I'll let you know. I don't want to cut off my prospects too quick," she grinned.

A week later, and two months after the incident at the school, Yellowhenry was served with the notice that he was being sued by the school district. He notified his boss in Helena who sent the notice to the Attorney General's office. A quick reply was directed to the school district informing them of the statutes which protected the highway patrol and its officers from frivolous lawsuits. The suit was quickly withdrawn.

The head of the patrol, Dennis Miles, then placed a call to Yellowhenry. "Trooper Joe," he began jovially, "tell me about this warning you gave the school about snakes in classrooms. Usually, that falls into keeping terrariums in classrooms for the kids to study. You know, how snakes shed their skins or how they eat rodents. That kind of thing. So what was your concern?"

"Dennis, would you want your kids to sit in front of a man handling, barehanded, fully envenomated rattlesnakes with no barrier, whatsoever, between the handler and the kids? Snakes freecrawling all over the guy."

"Hell, no. Is that really what they were doing?"

"Yes. For the past five years," Yellowhenry replied. "I told them to knock it off last year. Well, this year, bigger than hell, the snake handler and the teacher got into a pissing contest after a snake was dropped and stampeded the kids out of the room. The handler captured the snake, but when the teacher refused to pay him for the presentation, he tossed a different snake at the teacher. That was the first bite, the second occurred as the snake headed for the door and bit a girl who hadn't cleared the classroom because she was knocked nearly unconscious by the stampede of the kids running from the dropped snake.

"The tossed snake hit the hallway and refused to cooperate with the handler when he tried to capture it. So, what does he do? Pulls out a ten inch knife and entices the snake to strike. Split its head in two right between the venom sacks. Handler leaves the building with the snake going crazy in the hallway. When I got there, the damned thing was crawling away. I slapped a garbage can over it and had a Havre city policeman, who was the first on site, go get a shovel from the custodian. We killed the snake and tossed it into the school's incinerator."

"Jesus Christ," Miles exclaimed. "Are the idiots in charge up there?"

"Well, I called the principal a damned fool. Didn't make him happy."

"Is that handler in jail?"

"He was. He's out, now. He is a licensed herpetologist who has a snake ranch out of town toward Shelby. Sells snake venom. He has to be there all the time to take care of the stock."

"The stock? That's an interesting way to put it," Miles said with a shudder in his voice. "Damned rattlers give me the gooseflesh."

"I went out to the handler's place. A native by the name of Charlie Goodwoman. His prize snake, a big sonofabitch he called Bo got inside the frame of my car. He couldn't get back out and the mechanics at the shop refused to try and remove him until he was dead. Car still smells."

"How the hell did he get in there, Joe?"

"From the trunk. Nobody had been at the place for four days. It was crawling with Charlie's snakes. Fifteen of those he calls milkers and wild rattlers that had come in because Charlie's mice got out. And bull snakes that were eatin' the rattlers. Ol' Bo was out in the yard. I damned near ran over him. Wish to Christ I had. Charlie caught him with the son of a bitch doing his best to bite him. We stashed him in the trunk while we worked on the hoorah in the shack. Took us a couple of hours to straighten the place out."

"Oh, my god, Joe. Were you handling those snakes?"

"Not me, Dennis. I sure shot the shit out of a bunch of 'em, though."

Miles laughed, "That's what I would have done, too. So, now what's going on?"

"Lawsuits. My god everybody involved is suing. It's dividing the community. The school board fired the principal and he's suing for wrongful dismissal. Every kid in that classroom is being represented individually or in a class action. The teacher, fella by the name of Peacock, would have been fired, but his being snakebit saved his job. He has a lawsuit against Goodwoman for all the good that'll do him. Charlie only has his five acres and a shack at Greasewood Junction. Peacock might get that, but Charlie will simply set up on the reservation and keep doing what he's been doing. I'm his best buddy, now, by the way."

Miles laughed again, "Lucky you. A crazy son of a bitch for a buddy and all the snake you can eat."

"Yeah, I just hope that's all it is," Yellowhenry chuckled.

"Is there something else going on?"

"He comes into town twice a month and stays overnight. My neighbor is a widow who feeds him and washes his clothes while he takes a shower. Then he chases her around the house naked while his clothes dry. She comes over to my place if it gets too bad. He sleeps in my horse barn before he heads back to Greasewood Junction the next morning."

"Joe, this is just a horseback hunch, but watch that man. He sounds unbalanced to me."

"Well, he could be an armed man, but not with a gun," Yellowhenry mused. "A man armed with a snake. I'll keep an eye out, boss. I surely will."

Chapter 5

Yellowhenry and his stepson, ten year old James, were on a deer hunt into Wild Horse Basin. James was riding his two year old riding mule, Miracle, and his stepfather was riding his sorrel gelding, Hi Boy. They trailed a pack mule named Bray. The mule the boy was riding was a product of a wild stallion and a jenny, quite a rare occurrence since mules are normally sterile. It sparked the boy's naming his mule, Miracle. Yellowhenry had bought the animal for his son from their tribe which owned the mother. As they rode they chit chatted.

"Dad, do you think Mom will ever take a shit in our house?" James asked in reference to a promise Yellowhenry had broken to his wife, Amy, when he tried to delay putting in a septic tank and running water into their home. She was angered to the point of swearing she'd never use her husband's commode. Even though he'd relented and had installed everything right away, including adding Minnie Graves to an oversized tank and drain field, his wife, in three years, had never used the one in their house. She used their old outhouse or Minnie's commode.

"Well, she is more stubborn than I thought she would be about it, Son. I gave up asking why? But it's kept me keeping all my promises," Yellowhenry chuckled.

"It's weird. The kids at school thinks she crazy."

"James, that's a family secret. How did the kids find out?"

"It wasn't me. Susie spilled her guts when her teacher gave prizes for the best kept family secrets. Susie couldn't resist. I guess it was the best one, though."

"Does Mom know Susie told?"

"Oh, yeah. Susie bawled like a baby she felt so guilty. Mom told her it was okay."

"Really? And Mom still uses Minnie's bathroom?"

"Yeah. The kids tease Susie about her crazy mom. So, why does Mom keep doing that?"

"I'll ask her when we get back home. How'll that be?"

"Okay, but I think Mom should knock it off because if those kids keep after Susie, I'm gonna kick some ass."

"Well, I know you're protective toward your sister, James, but beating up those kids isn't something you should do. Think of all the problems that will cause and ask yourself if any solutions to those problems will occur as you're beating ass. You know, problems that would cause for me and Mom, problems with you and your school, with those kids' parents, with those kids' older brothers and sisters who would come after your ass."

"It isn't fair, Dad. What would you do?"

"I'd realize it's a problem it will take help to solve, or to at least make better. It may never be solved, Son. But over time and with some assistance, it will get better."

"Okay, but Joey Silverstream is gonna get a knuckle sandwich."

"He, I take it, is the worst one."

"Yeah, if he'd shut up, the rest of 'em would, too."

"Silverstream?" Yellowhenry said, musing. "Joey has an older brother or two, doesn't he?"

"Three, but I don't care. They don't bother Susie. Joey does."

"Aren't you afraid they'll bother you, though, if you punch out their little brother?"

"Yeah, Dad. I'm afraid. But I'll do it anyway."

"Let's hold onto your solution as a last resort, James, okay?"

"I'll try, Dad, but that Joey is a mean damned shit. And not just to Susie, either. The teachers think they can sweet talk him into stopping it. But I know they can't. He likes it. That's the problem. He likes it."

"Isn't he in your room?"

"Yeah, but his sister is in Susie's and she told Joey."

"And he doesn't give you a bad time about it?"

"Both Susie and I get it, Dad. And some of the other kids follow Joey."

"Okay, son. Maybe I have an idea that might help."

"What is it?"

"Have you heard of the Police Athletic League in Havre?"

"Sort of."

"They teach boxing, Judo, and wrestling," Yellowhenry said. "Have you thought about taking up one of those?"

"No."

"Do you think you might?"

"Judo, Dad. I'd really like to do that."

"All right. That's step one of our solution."

The pair spent two days deer hunting but didn't find a buck that Yellowhenry would take. James was only carrying a .22 and he bagged a rabbit each day that they ate with their evening meals. Yellowhenry showed his son how to pack the big mule and balance the load so the animal's back didn't get sore. That night as they sat at their campfire, he also told him the story of how he'd fallen off a rock face, dislocating his knee, and how he'd spent ten days at the head of the Wild Horse drainage repairing and resting his knee so he could walk out. "That bearskin rug you kids roll out came from that trip."

"Is that the trip when you found Hi Boy?"

"You could call it that, but really he found me. He was just skin and bones when we teamed up."

"How did you fatten him up?"

"It was easy. He just needed to have his teeth floated. With good hay, oats, and Minnie's love, he bounced back in no time," Yellowhenry smiled. "Well, I had him wormed, too."

"Dad, we dissected horse worms in science class at school. They were long, colorless, and mostly a tube within a tube. Are those what Hi Boy shit out?"

"Well, his were pink, but the rest of it fits. You could go fishin' with his worms."

"Yech," James expressed. "I'll pass. I can't imagine shittin' a worm like that. Can you?"

"Well, if I did, I'm sure Mom would never use our commode."

James giggled, "Neither would I, Dad. Do you ever feel bad about killing Hi Boy's previous owner, Dad?"

"Yes, James. I do. It never should have happened."

"Why did it?"

"The man sold Hi Boy to me and then tried to steal him back. When the police tried to arrest him, he began shooting. I was there and he shot at me. I managed to get my hands on the officer's shotgun. When the man kept shooting at the officer, I returned fire."

"Was the officer killed?"

"No. The man was shooting pheasant loads. The officer's shotgun was loaded with buckshot. There's no comparson between the damage number six shot causes and the damage double ought buckshot causes, Son."

"What is the difference?"

"The officer had pellets in his ass and back that they removed down at the clinic. My shots blew splinters from the man's door frame clear through his chest and out his back."

"Wow. Did he die right away?"

"He did. Later, I brought his son who was wanted for murder in out of the Moose's Ass. My testimony for him saved him from the death penalty. When the man's younger brother stole Hi Boy and Jay and Bray, he wanted to kill me. He got away up toward the Moose's Ass and got stomped by a cow moose. You know the story of Liam Greene. He works at the General Store. I brought him back on a travois. He and I are good friends, now. Doesn't make up for killing Horace, though. I regret that every time I think of it."

James sat very still, thinking about wooden splinters blowing through a man's back. Finally, he asked, "Dad, could you have rocked that man?" The reference was to Yellowhenry's reknown for throwing egg sized rocks at ninety miles an hour with unerring accuracy. It was how he collected small game animals and birds for his campfire. He had also used the skill on a few men to subdue them in lieu of shooting them with his firearm.

"Yes, James, and if he hadn't been shooting, I might have. But I had no idea what load he was shooting. He could have killed Officer Abernathy with a little heavier load. Number four duck and goose loads would have been heavy enough to do it from the distance they were apart. It just turned into a shit show from hell. Don't tell your mother I said that."

James, grinned, "I won't. She might make me eat out on the porch."

"I wouldn't doubt it," Yellowhenry chuckled. "Well, let's roll out our bedrolls and get some shuteye."

Chapter 6

Yellowhenry and Amy, who was four months pregnant with her seventh baby, his fourth, were lieing in bed following sex as they discussed family and his and Jame's hunting trip. "You know, you're about to get your breeding priveleges cut off," she said.

"I know," he said. "I just love your babies, sweetheart."

"I know you do, but I've had one every year we've been married. I'm getting tired, Joe."

"I'll make a deal with you," he said.

"Let's make a deal? That used to be a game show on television. Didn't always work out for the contestant, though. Is that what you have in mind for me?"

"Sort of. It's a twofer, though."

"What, twofer you and nought for Amy?"

He reached his hand to her face and turned her to him so he could kiss her deeply.

"Nooo," he said slowly, drawing it out. "I wouldn't mind a twofer tonight, though. What do you think?"

"I want to hear your deal first."

"First, you'll get my vasectomy. Second, you start using the commode here in the house."

She sat bolt upright, "You know how I feel about that," she exclaimed. "What brought that up?"

"James did," he said calmly. "He's about to fight Joey Silverstream over it."

"Susie told the secret and now she's being teased, isn't she?"

"Fraid so, but so is James. He gets it from Joey and his buddies."

"That won't change if I start using our commode, though, Joe."

"Honey, it will help because the kids can laugh and say that it was true, but it isn't anymore. That will take some pressure off. I'm also putting James into Judo classes with the Police Athletic League."

"So, why won't Joey jump into Judo when he finds out?"

"It's a program that requires a fee. The Silverstreams won't pay for something like that. Jame's plan is to give Joey a knuckle sandwich."

"Tell him, 'no way,' Joe," she exclaimed. "His older brothers would attack James. He could really get hurt."

"Honey, that's why I want him in Judo classes. He will have a much better chance to defend himself if he knows how to do it."

"If they jump James, I'm going to beat the shit out of Audrey," she claimed hotly.

Yellowhenry couldn't help himself, he guffawed loudly. "Mom?" Susie's voice came wafting through the door. "What's the matter with Dad?"

"Nothing, honey. Go back to sleep."

"I wanna see," the little girl said suddenly opening her parents bedroom door. Amy barely had time to cover herself before her daughter crawled into bed beside her.

"Okay, honey," Amy whispered to her husband. "I'm on your crapper, but no twofer for you tonight."

"Dang, craps again," he whispered, grinning happily.

It took the winter for James to develop his Judo skills. He had turned eleven on his last birthday and had gone through a growth spurt in which he grew two inches and gained fourteen pounds. As a fifth grader, he was athletic and muscular. Three times a week, he worked and trained at the Havre PAL. His trainer happened to be Roland Hainlign. The fervor with which James approached perfecting the skills he was being taught made Hainlign take time to speak to Yellowhenry. He had taken some video on his cell phone of James in training.

Yellowhenry watched his stepson and was surprised at how intensely he finished throws, sweeps, and body strikes. "Damn, Roland, if I were in my son's class, he's the last kid I'd tangle with."

"He is burning inside with the desire not to defend but to inflict pain and injury, Joe. We have to discontinue his training. We can't get other kids in his group to train with him, and the law forbids us from moving him up to bigger kids. He is capable of that, however. I'm sorry, but you'll have to hire a private tutor or put him in a private gym."

"I see that, Roland. It looks like he's good enough right now to be dangerous to the average kid of his own age."

"That's sort of why I wanted to talk to you. Maybe you could talk to James and explain that Judo is a time honored martial art for self defense not for attacking others," Hainlign said.

"Thanks for alerting me, Roland. Do me a favor and forward that video to me. I need him, his mother, and his sister to see this."

"Will do Captain. Sorry for the bad news."

Chapter 7

The family meeting took place the following evening. With all four involved family members gathered at the kitchen table, Yellowhenry began. "James, you're just too good. Take a look at this."

Amy blurted, "James, you're trying to hurt those kids."

"Mom, it's Judo. Those are the moves I'm being taught."

"Were being taught, Son. I spoke to Officer Hainlign yesterday. The kids you were training with have bowed out. They won't train with you anymore. Seems that instead of learning the moves for self defense, you are learning them to attack. That's why you finish the moves with what looks like anger."

James sat quietly picking at his fingernails. The table was silent until Susie said, "James, don't kick his ass until I can watch."

"Susie," Amy exclaimed. "What are you saying?"

"Mom!" James shouted. "You don't know what a shit Joey Silverstream is. Susie and I have waited all winter until I was ready. Well, now I am."

"James, we signed you up so you could learn how to defend yourself," Yellowhenry said sternly.

"Okay, Dad. Let me tell you what he does. He walks past my desk every day and whispers, 'Yelladick, you're just a pussy.' If he wants to sharpen a pencil, he walks past my desk and if Mrs. Wainwright isn't watching, he hits the back of my head with a knuckle shot. If he sees Susie in the hall, he just accidentally shoulders her into the wall, or accidentally knocks her books to the floor. Then Alvin Horsman tells her to keep her mouth shut, or else. In the cafeteria, he'll grab something off my tray or just shove the tray at me. Every week he comes up with something else. Susie and I have made a pact. That's all I'm going to say."

"Joe, you have to go to school and get this straightened out," Amy said vehemently. "Or I'll take care of it."

"All right, now all of you listen to me," Yellowhenry said sternly. "James, you will not attack Joey Silverstream or Alvin Horsman. You are only to defend yourself and your sister. Do you hear me, James. Defense only. Tomorrow is Monday. My schedule won't allow me to go talk to the principal until Thursday. Now, in P.E. basketball you are not to defensively leg sweep those boys, or defensively hip check them into the bleachers, or accidentally and defensively strike them in the body with your elbows. Is that clear?"

James glanced up at his stepfather to see just how 'for real' his speech was. Yellowhenry winked at him while maintaining a solemn face. "Yeah, I get it Dad. Defense only," he said, with a small grin he kept from his mother.

"If one more thing happens, I'm taking over," Amy gritted while staring at her husband. "There's no hope for you doing anything about it."

"Well, I'm tied up till Thursday, so if you can get Minnie in here to take care of the little ones, you can go talk to Mr. Goldman before then," Yellowhenry said, sudden anger rising in his retort.

"That's not what I had in mind," she fired back.

"Well, then you and I need to talk without the kids here."

James and Susie left and Amy folded her arms over her stomach. "Okay, Joe. Tell me what I already know. It's up to me."

"Not going to waste my time with that," he said angrily. "I need you to figure out with Minnie and your mother how much to pay them to take care of our kids for several days. You know, in case you're injured in some way, or get arrested and taken to jail for assault and battery. I'll bail you out as soon as I can, but it could be forty-eight hours, or so. Get the house stocked up with food, diapers stacked, and so on. We'll need to get some formula because you won't be able to nurse Waylon. What am I leaving out here? Come on, now. You aren't helping."

"You're just being a smart ass. There's no help for that."

"And you're being stupid. There's no help for that, either."

"Shall we start shouting, now, Joe?"

"Shout all you want. I won't be here to listen to it."

"Oh, great. Take off like you always do. Do you want me to pack you food for a week?" she said to his back as he went into their bedroom. He didn't answer as he pulled down a suitcase and began packing it with clothing he would wear in the field. She followed him and watched from the door. "That isn't what you take on your horse. Where are you going?"

He continued what he was doing silently, adding his shaving kit and hygiene stuff along with a toothbrush. Then, he reached into the closet and pulled from the overhead shelf a locked pistol safe. He worked the combination and removed his backup pistol, a Colt .45. He placed it with two boxes of ammunition and a shoulder holster he pulled from inside the closet in his suitcase, closed it, and set it on the floor. He returned the pistol safe to the shelf and turned to his wife. "There's been a prison break from Deer Lodge. We've been asked to send a deputy down for the manhunt. I'm taking the assignment myself. I'm driving down tonight. You can check with the office if you're interested in updates. If you want to punch Audrey Silverstream in the nose, go ahead. I'd never be able to stop you, anyway."

Amy's resolve suddenly started to waver. "Joe, don't go because you're mad at me, please." She began apologetically, "Send a deputy. I'm sorry, Joe. I didn't mean what I said. I just didn't think because I'm so tired of James and Susie being bullied."

"Wait till Thursday. James has a handle on that," he said, picking up the suitcase. Without saying anything more, he picked up his service belt and left the house. He tossed the suitcase and belt into the backseat of his cruiser. Amy followed him out to the car.

"Joe, don't leave without saying goodbye. Please, Joe," she pleaded. "I love you so much."

He looked at her strangely as though he was seeing her for the first time without love. He leaned down and brushed his lips to hers and said, "Goodbye Amy."

Chapter 8

James was backpedaling as Alvin Horsman dribbled the basketball straight at him with the obvious intent of simply running him down. James checked over his shoulder and angled toward the sideline. Horsman followed grinning as he picked up speed. Just before he collided with James, the target suddenly dropped down, turned with the dribbler and seemingly without effort deposited him into the bleachers at the edge of the court.

James grabbed the loose ball and headed back up court. Joey Silverstream raced at him from his right intending to bowl him over. James checked his dribble and Joey flashed by in front of him only to find his feet inextricably tangled. He dove headfirst into the bottom riser of the last seat of the bleachers. James continued with his dribble before passing to a baseline cutting teammate who laid the ball into the basket on a very pretty play. Mr. Millhouse, the P.E. teacher blew his whistle to stop play. "That was really nice," he shouted. "Way to go." Then, he checked on the pair slowly recovering from their encounters with the bleachers.

"He tripped me," Joey cried. He was holding his left hand over his split left eyebrow as blood poured with his tears to the floor.

"He hipped me into the bleachers," Alvin shouted running at James. "Put 'em up, Yelladick."

Instead James spun and hip threw his antagonist over his shoulder. Alvin spilled to the floor on his back with the wind knocked from his lungs. He lay gasping as the stunned class gaped at the bully with tears coursing from his eyes as he tried to suck in oxygen.

"That's enough," Millhouse roared. "Everyone to the locker room. Joey, wait here till I get a towel. I don't want blood all over the gym."

"James, see if you can help Alvin. I'll be right back."

When the teacher and class had cleared the floor, James walked over to Joey. "That was Judo, dickhead. I'll throw you into every wall in this school if that's the way you want it. Understand? I know twenty-eight Judo moves. I promise you I'll use them all on you if you say one more nasty thing to Susie or me. I'll come huntin' ya, you miserable prick. And I'll love every second of it."

"I won't do anything else, James," Joey sniffled. "I promise."

"You call me Yelladick again, and I'll catch you after school. Bring your brothers while you're at it. I'll take them on, too."

"I'm done, James. No more of that shit from me."

Alvin was getting some of his breath back when James walked to him and used the heel of his hand to punch him in the solar plexus, returning him to gasping like a fish out of water. "Hey, buttface," James said leaning into his face. "Listen up. In case you were too busy suckin' for air, I used three Judo moves on you. There's plenty more where that came from. So, drop the bullshit with me and my sister. You got that?"

Alvin made a noise as he nodded his head while he turned and heaved for breath. "I'll take that as a 'yes' for now. After you start breathin', come tell me what you really think. I can't wait to hear it."

Just then Millhouse came walking quickly with a towel, "Isn't Alvin breathing yet? Here, Joey, hold this to your eye. James, help me get Alvin to his feet."

Alvin had finally gotten his diaphragm reset and was sucking in air in gasps. Millhouse took his left arm while James gripped his right. He pressed a pair of fingers into the brachial nerve, causing Alvin to shriek and jerk his arm, but James grip at the elbow held fast. "What's wrong?" Millhouse asked, alarmed.

"He's hurting my arm, he's hurting my arm!" Alvin shrieked.

James stopped pressing as Millhouse demanded, "What are you doing?"

"I think he hurt his arm somehow when he fell, Mr. Millhouse, didn't you, Alvin?" James said more than asked as he eased off the pressure.

"Yeah, I think so," he answered miserably. "It feels better, now."

Millhouse wrote both boys up on disciplinary referrals. James spent his hour after school in the detention room working on homework and eyeballing Alvin Horsman. Alvin saw James grinning at him and looked away quickly each time. When the boys were released, Alvin hurried away without a word.

Jame's reputation spread like wildfire. All the boys wanted to be his friend and learn his moves. He just smiled and became buddies. He never shared his Judo skills with any of them.

Amy was torn in two directions. Relief that her kids were no longer the subjects of bullying, and a haunting concern that her husband, in a twinkling, had somehow fallen out of love with her. His emotionally vacant parting as he suddenly plunged off in a last second decision following one of their spats into a dangerous assignment he would normally have assigned to one of his deputies, had her worried that it was her fault. She knew that, at times, his C type psychological profile made him crave solitude and distance from others. He was usually given, however, to saddling his horse, packing a mule, and riding into the back country for a long weekend. He would come back refreshed and ready to take up his role as father, husband, and Captain of the Havre, Montana

Highway Patrol office. She even pushed him to go sometimes when she sensed he was getting owly. Even his Indian nickname, Sand in his Shoes, was descriptive of that personality trait in his character.

Except for one other angry moment, however, when he had left after one of their disagreements as he'd set off to hunt a grizzly bear, did he leave without telling her he loved her as his parting statement. For that he had apologized and asked her forgiveness. This latest parting was entirely different. He had simply gone, leaving the moment empty of emotion. She didn't know what to think, but the unknown was unsettling when she had time to reflect on the strange expression on her husband's face and the mechanical way he had said goodbye without telling her he loved her.

Yellowhenry drove toward Deer Lodge through the long dark night mostly on cruise control. Strangely, his parting from his wife, brought on by a last second decision, which could have been made out of anger was not. He'd just decided he needed something to do besides routine. It should have bothered him that he'd brushed off Amy the way he did, but it didn't. He wasn't even sure why. He was more interested in the outcome of his instructing James to take down the school bullies.

The usual four hours it took to drive from Havre to Deer Lodge took Yellowhenry six. He'd taken a coffee break in a small town just southeast of Great Falls. The Cascade Mountains Café was owned and operated by a thirty year old divorced woman from Randle, Washington. Monti Collier was five feet, four inches tall with black hair and emerald colored eyes. Her one hundred ten pounds were packed on a sensuous and well endowed frame. Facially, she was quite attractive except for a somewhat oversized nose that was a bit beak- like. "What can I do ya for, officer?"

she asked Yellowhenry who eased down into a booth past the big picture window that fronted the highway. He was the only customer in the place.

"Coffee, black," he sighed.

She walked to the front and flipped off the neon sign mounted on the roof outside, turned the open sign to closed, and closed the shuttered window shade on the glass fronted door which she locked. Then, she walked behind the breakfast counter, grabbed a coffee pot and two cups, and joined Yellowhenry. She sat down opposite him and poured the coffee. "On the house," she smiled cheerily. "I'm just closing up."

"That's not necessary," he returned, smiling at the open and friendly face of his sudden companion. "I don't mean to keep you open."

"Well, it's my honor, Trooper Joe," she said.

"Wow, you know who I am?" he asked in disbelief.

"You're the most famous and interesting lawman in the state of Montana. I'm very proud that you've stopped at my little place of business. I hope you don't mind my using your visit to enhance my restaurant."

"Be my guest," he smiled. "I can't see how it would make a difference, but use my name if it helps."

"So, what brings the Havre Montana State police captain down here? You headed to Helena for something?"

"No," he said. "Prison break at Deer Lodge. It's been on the radio the last couple of days."

"Hmmm, that got by me. I guess they didn't come this way for coffee, huh?"

He laughed, "Well, they missed something good. You make a perfect cup of coffee."

"Ha!" she exclaimed. "That's what I'm going to use. 'Trooper Joe says I make a perfect cup of Joe.' Is that okay with you?"

"Sure, whatever," he smiled. "By the way, how did you come by the name of your restaurant?"

"Well, my name is Monti, which my father assures me, means mountain. I'm from the Cascade Mountains of Washington State, and this town is named Cascade. So it all just seemed to fit."

"That painting on your back wall must be Mt. Rainier, I take it."

She grinned, "Nope, it's Mt. Adams. I had it painted there because it's a conversation starter. People who don't know Adams usually guess Rainier or Mt. Baker. So, I get them to talking about the Cascades. We get friendly. Where it really shows up is in my tips."

"Very clever. If you're from that part of the country, what brings you here?" he asked.

"Love," she answered simply.

"Oh," he said. "I didn't mean to pry. I did notice you aren't wearing rings."

"Divorced. My husband found himself a cowgirl and they rode off into the sunset."

"I'm sorry," he said.

"Don't be. We weren't happy after the first year. It happens. Are you looking for a girlfriend," she grinned.

"What? You want to come riding into the sunrise?" he laughed.

"I'd sure do that with you, if you'd give me the chance," she hooted.

"Well, I must tell you, that a few years ago, I would have been here with an extra horse."

"What's wrong with now?" she said looking into his eyes.

"Monti, I'm married with six kids."

"Happily?"

"Well, not especially at the moment."

"Perfect opportunity for some consoling. My apartment is upstairs. Let's take the coffee up there."

"I should get going," he said.

"Shush. Let's get out of the restaurant before someone else wants to stop for coffee."

Yellowhenry felt himself being pulled along by primal instinct, fairly certain that he had control of the situation. She sat him on her sofa and freshened his coffee cup. "Put your legs up on the coffee table," she said. "I'll be right back." She moved quickly to a bedroom door and disappeared. Yellowhenry sipped his coffee and looked around. The apartment contained many feminine touches, but framed prints of the Cascades were in evidence in several places. The walls were painted in a soft muted matte green. The furniture was an eclectic collection of oak, mahogany, and maple pieces. There were no sawdust furnishings.

She returned a few minutes later, wearing a white, slinky see-through, knee length nightgown. She was sans bra and panties. Yellowhenry's eyes shot to the dark triangle at the top of her thighs. He knew immediately that he was not in control of the situation. Her perfume touched him first as he set his coffee cup on the table and dropped his legs to the floor. She settled in beside him and they kissed. Then, to her surprise, he stood up, thanked her for her hospitality, and left.

Chapter 9

An hour later, his lust diminished, Yellowhenry berated himself, but in the back of his mind he toyed with the idea of a return trip for coffee. Monti had assured him he would be most welcome despite the incomplete tryst that stalled her hopes and plans.

After checking in with the task force in charge of apprehending the escapees, Yellowhenry went to the motel set up for participating lawmen. Monti's perfume was still a caress in his hair and on his uniform. He took a shower and hung his uniform jacket and pants in the closet to air out. After a few hours of sleep, he dressed in camoflauge and went back to the command center.

The man in charge was from the Missoula office of the FBI. Dolan Aimes was known to Yellowhenry as the man in charge of an unsolved murder case that originated in Missoula and ended in Wisconsin. Three bank robbers had kidnapped a woman and her college aged daughter and raped them for several days before the women escaped. One of the three criminals had been killed at the site of the escape by the older brother of the other two. The brothers had been killed in Wisconsin by the mother, but Aimes had not been able to prove it, and after strong spoken encouragement by his superior in the Missoula office, had cold filed the case. He wasn't over it, however.

"Trooper Joe," Aimes exclaimed. "I was expecting a deputy. It's very good to see you, though."

"Hello, Dolan," Yellowhenry said. "It's been quite awhile."

"Yeah," Aimes said. "Ever since that robbery, rape, and murder case. It has been cold case filed, but I know that mother shot those two just as sure as I'm sitting here."

"Maybe, maybe not," Yellowhenry smiled. "Either way, they got what they deserved."

"That's what Director Devisiter told me. I don't disagree, but I'm always bothered when there's a shoe in the air on a case."

"Well, Dolan, there are more shoes in the air than a man can shake a stick at. I'd just let that one float out there."

"Yeah, I get it. Joe, on this case I want you to team up with Stanley Whitedeer. There were five in the bunch that broke out. We've caught two, but the other three are Kootenai and Flathead Indians. We think there's a good chance they are being aided by the Native Americans in the Swan Valley. In addition to English, those people up there speak the Salish language. Stanley does, too. Do you?"

"Afraid not. Cree and English."

"Okay, but with your experience and Stanley to interpret, you are the best team we have to look into that country. While we wait for him to get here, you can take a look at the files we have on the escapees."

The first file was that of a thirty-five year old Kootenai Indian named Kenny Lost Deer. He was in the eleventh year of a thirty year sentence for murder. He had whacked his neighbor over a property boundary line dispute. Both men owned adjacent off reservation property on the Clark Fork River. The neighbor had moved survey markers to steal forty feet of Lost Deer's riverfront property. Lost Deer's response was to simply empty a handgun into the neighbor, throw his body into the river, and reset the markers. Other than that, he had no criminal history.

The second file was on a fifty year old mixed blood member of the Flatheads named Henry Shot Once. His file was extensive and it was clear to Yellowhenry that the man was a professional criminal. With only six months to go on a three year hitch for running a chop shop, it was clear that prison was considered by Shot Once as business interruption.

The final file was more ominous. G.A. Smith was in for distribution of drugs, including fentanyl, into various Indian reservations as well as into the University of Montana in Missoula, and Montana State University in Bozeman. He had connections to the Sinaloa Cartel out of Mexico. He had just begun a ten year stint. It was suspected that he was the ringleader who had orchestrated the breakout with unidentified assistance from outside the prison. Smith was a half breed of Mexican and Comanche heritage. He was a thirty-seven year old illegal immigrant.

His most identifying features were a patch over his left eye and the loss of his left ear.

Yellowhenry's perusal had just completed when Stanley Whitedeer came striding in. Yellowhenry looked up and up and up. At nearly seven feet tall, and three hundred fifty-nine pounds, he was the largest man Yellowhenry had ever seen. He possessed a deep bass voice that came out as a near growl. "Trooper Joe," he said, holding out a mitt that swallowed Yellowhenry's hand clear to his wrist. "I am honored to be selected to work with you." He smiled, revealing an uneven set of small, discolored and misshapen teeth. It seemed to add to his visage as that of a human bear.

"Well, thank you," Yellowhenry stammered, still taking in the mammoth standing before him. "Have you seen the files on the guys we're after?"

"I have. Smith, we'll never see. Cartel's got him over the border by now. Of the other two, Shot Once is a lowlife skunk. As for Lost Deer, he did what I woulda done before I joined the patrol. Shot Once is just an idiot, but he'll shoot at ya if you get too close. They'll hang together as far as Kalispell, then they'll go separate ways. Lost Deer has family and property on the Clark Fork. Good chance he'll be headin' there. Shot Once could go anywhere."

"Should we start at Kalispell, then?"

"They won't be there for a couple of weeks, or so," Whitedeer answered. "Once there, it's big enough they could disappear within the population. Our best bet is to sort them out in the Swan Valley. Very few people in those parts. I just hope they don't cross over into the Bob Marshall Wilderness. We'd have a bitch of a time in there."

Chapter 10

Before joining Whitedeer, Yellowhenry called his office in Havre to place his sergeant, Art McClintock in charge until further notice. "Your wife called," the front desk officer, Barbara Premminger said. "She'd like you to call her."

"Do me a favor, Barbara," Yellowhenry said. "Call and tell her I'm leaving for the field and will have to call later."

"Will do, Captain. Stay safe out there." Barbara Premminger was an officer from the Cree Reservation. She had worked for Yellowhenry when he was the sheriff of the reservation police force. She had followed him when an opening on the MHP came up due to a retirement.

The vehicle the pair used to drive north to the Swan Valley was an old roundtop '1952 Ford F-100 with the headliner removed. Whitedeer grinned as he took the wheel. "What do you think, Joe? This is my state issue. Undercover. Lowered seat. I don't fit into anything else."

"How the hell did you qualify at your height? The state patrol has always had an upward limit."

"I grew after I got on, so out here in the boonies, they made an exception."

"You grew what? Six inches?"

"Eight!" Whitedeer's laugh was an odd bass cackle.

Yellowhenry glanced at him. "Wow," he said. "What office are you connected with?"

"Libby."

"Ah, Libby. That explains it," Yellowhenry muttered.

"What's that?" Whitedeer asked.

"Oh, nothing."

Several hours later, they pulled into the Cenex Gas Station in Seeley Lake at the southern end of the Swan Valley. Both officers, dressed in jeans and camo, stepped out of the rig. While Whitedeer gassed up, Yellowhenry looked around and stretched out his butt and back. A resident pulled in to get gas and gawked at Whitedeer. Yellowhenry was leaning against the fender of the offside of the pickup. The man looked at him and whispered sotto voice, "You with him?"

"Uh, huh."

"We see Indians around here all the time, but not one that size. Hell, they ain't nobody round here that big. You fellas just passing through?"

"Maybe. Hard to tell. You say you see Indians around all the time. Is that because you're being nice to us Indians?"

"No, no. I ain't racist," the man said.

"Good. We're looking for another pair of Indians who came through here, probably three days back. One of 'em is wanted for murder."

"Murder! You mean there's murderin' Indians loose around here?"

"Possibly. Have you seen or heard of a couple of 'em?"

"I heard there was a couple of suspicious lookin' types. In fact, I heard there was a stolen pickup that disappeared couple of nights ago. That has to explain it. I'll be goddamned. What's this country comin' to?"

"Damned if I know. Indians allowed to run loose. Say, do you know where the local cop might be?"

"Office is at city hall. Four blocks up north and two off to the right. Hardly ever there, though."

"Yeah. The Indians probably won't be either."

"You pullin' my leg?"

"No, no," Yellowhenry smiled. "I mean the only reason for that would be if they'da been jailed. You woulda known that, right?"

"Of course, I woulda known," the man said. "Who wouldn't?"

"Good point. Nice talk," Yellowhenry said as the man hung the gas nozzle back on the pump.

"Yeah, sure," the resident said as he started up his rig. "Let me give you some advice. You two need to follow your buddies. Keep on movin'."

"Did you learn anything from the yokel?" Whitedeer rumbled when the pair drove away from the station.

"Stolen pickup couple of nights ago."

"We need to find the local gendarme, then," Whitedeer said.

They found the city policeman at a coffee shop. Michael Willis, like everyone else, gave Whitedeer the carnival gawk. "So, you fellas are with the patrol, eh?"

"We are," Yellowhenry said. "We're interested in a stolen pickup a couple of nights ago. Was there another vehicle dumped somewhere in town?"

"Now that you mention it, there's a blue Kia SUV I tagged just off the main drag. It's scheduled to be towed tomorrow morning. If you want to take a look at it, I can take you to it."

"Let's go," Whitedeer said.

"Huh?" Willis asked.

"Let's go, he said," Yellowhenry helped.

"Okay, I didn't catch that. Problem with my ears. Low notes run together on me," Willis explained.

The Kia SUV was locked. The men walked around it, trying to shade their eyes to get better looks inside. Suddenly the driver's side window exploded. Whitedeer looked at the two on the passenger side. "I stumbled. Tried to catch myself but my elbow ran through the window. I'm okay, though."

Yellowhenry walked around and said, "Well, we might just as well look inside while we're here."

"Don't you need a search warrant first?" Willis asked.

"We would if we were looking to file charges. We aren't. The guys we're after won't need to defend against these charges," Whitedeer stated.

Willis looked at Yellowhenry quizzically. "The escapees won't be defending against illegal search and seizure. That is immaterial." Whitedeer reached inside and popped the doorlocks. Soon the car was opened, doors and hatchback.

"Call your wrecker, Mike," Yellowhenry said a few moments later. He lifted the spare tire hatch cover in the back of the car. He pulled from the compartment three orange jumpsuits the backs of which were stenciled with Deer Lodge Penitentiary identification.

"Smith was with 'em when they stole this car," Whitedeer said. "He ditched the jumpsuit and joined the cartel boys who had clothes for all of them. Our guys came north and Smith went south."

"Thanks for your help, Mike," Yellowhenry said, shaking hands with the city marshal. When Willis shook hands with Whitedeer, his hand couldn't span the big man's palm. It was a clumsy flop both men grinned about.

Willis gave the officers the description of the stolen pickup. A black three year old Toyota Tacoma that had been parked in front of a residence with the keys left in the ignition.

The drive north up the Swan Valley was scenic with many small roadside lakes tucked into mature pine, fir, and tamarack stands of timber along with interspersing deciduous aspen, willow, and cottonwood groves. Side roads led out to ranches, cabins, and other lakes from small to medium size. Cattle and horse pastures were fenced alongside the roads. Campgrounds were featured at most lakes, and private cabins and property were common as well.

The officers began by cruising all the campgrounds and running out all the side roads on both sides of the two lane highway that bisected the wide river valley. It was nearing nightfall when they hit the Holland Lake turnoff to the 400 acre lake that lay at the base of the Swan Range mountains that separated it and the Bob Marshall Wilderness. There were a pair of Forest Service campgrounds on separate loops along the northern edge of the lake. Private property was located on the opposite side, and Holland Lake Lodge was located close to the head of the lake against the flank of the mountains.

The pair ran both campground loops before checking with the camp host. Webb Gaines and his wife Heather were a retired couple who had signed up to care for campgrounds because they were bored with retirement. They were delighted with the Holland Lake assignment and were pleased and surprised to have the Mutt and Jeff duo of highway patrolman call on them at their forty foot travel trailer in which they lived during the camping season. "I take it you aren't looking for a campsite," Gaines said after the introductions.

"No, we noticed on the upper loop a tag on a post showing the site reserved for three more days, but no one was there and there was no camping gear around either," Yellowhenry said.

"That spot is taken all right," Heather said. "A pair of very polite Native American men sleep there at night in their pickup."

"Did they give you their names?" Whitedeer asked.

"Oh, yes. They have to do that," Heather answered. "One of them has a seasonal pass. Lynn Crane. The other is Norman Sorenson."

"I see," Yellowhenry said. "Is their pickup a black Toyota Tacoma?"

"Yeah, it is," Webb said. "How did you know that?"

"Oh, my god!" Heather exclaimed. "They stole that pickup, didn't they?"

"Among other things," Yellowhenry said grimly.

The breakout at Deer Lodge was orchestrated by the mid level soldiers of the Sinaloa Cartel. They had been ordered to either exterminate G.A. Smith or spring him. The order had come from the top echelon, perhaps from the office of Sinaloa's leader, El Chapo, itself. Whatever the level of authority, the prison break was set up. A pair of cars were stolen with stolen license plates installed. The Kia that went north and a Ford F-150 that spirited Smith south toward Mexico were the two vehicles.

The breakout itself occurred as a smooth process of greasing palms. A construction crew constituted step one. It was brought in to rebuild an aging exterior wall in an exercise yard. It was a ten day job and the demolition phase occurred on day four. A gap in the wall was left open. The prisoners who simply walked out were recruited by Smith. They were necessary to split law enforcement resources and to serve as a distraction to his own escape.

The walkout took place on a moonless night at three A.M. Guards had been paid exorbitant fees to accommodate the selected five. The guards involved disappeared before their next shifts began. Altogether, it was an expensive but bloodless escape. In the finger pointing that followed, it was ironically determined that guards at the prison were underpaid.

Shot Once and Lost Deer had ditched their Kia because it was nearly out of gas. After walking the darkened side streets of Seeley Lake they had found the black Tacoma unlocked with the keys in the ignition. They had stolen the pickup and headed north up the Swan Valley. "Damn," Shot Once said. "We need to find a way to get our hands on some money."

"Cabins," Lost Deer said. "Let's check out cabins. A lot of those recreational ones are still vacant. They have stuff we can run into Kalispell and hock or sell."

Shot Once looked at his cohort and grinned. "Well, I'll be damned, Kenny," he said. "You aren't just another pretty face, are you?"

"Hope not," Lost Deer chuckled. "Take a left on the road coming up. It leads to a lake that has private cabins on it."

The cabin they broke into yielded a pair of hunting rifles and ammunition to match which they kept. They trucked some pieces of artwork to Kalispell where they pawned it. With $250 dollars in their hip pockets, the pair began to feel like they were onto something. The next two days yielded five more break-ins and fifteen hundred dollars for each man. They found pawning guns to be particularly lucrative. Each had also scored a sidearm with holster and accompanying ammunition.

After they had been refused a pawn for the second time, the men decided they had to call it off. As a reward to themselves they gave up the campsite at the Holland Lake Campground they had been using to stay out of sight. Instead they drove to the lodge and rented a cabin. The luxury of a shower and a full sized bed was an unexpressed joy.

"Where are you headed, Kenny?" Shot Once asked.

"Got my own cabin down on the Clark Fork. Where are you headed?"

"Out of state. Not sure just where, yet. Maybe Arizona."

"Well," Lost Deer said, "one of us is gonna need a set of wheels."

"It's not a problem. The people up at the upper end of the valley are just as trusting as those in Seeley Lake. Hell, some of 'em don't even lock their doors at night."

"There's a rig pullin' up at the office," Lost Deer said. "Something about it bothers me. Take a look, Henry. Isn't that big bastard a cop?"

"What?" Shot Once said, hustling to the window. "Ah, shit! That's Stan Whitedeer. Famous up around Libby. That other guy is Joe Yellowhenry out of Havre. We must really be wanted to have those two on our asses. Let's let them go inside, then get the hell out of here."

When the men stepped out of their cabin, Shot Once glanced up the road and saw an MHP unit parked crosswise. He jerked back inside the cabin, shoving Lost Deer back as he did so. "What is it?" Lost Deer asked, alarmed.

"Highway Patrol has us blocked in here. I'm taking my rifle and headin' for the Bob. The trail's just up the ridge from here. If we hustle, we'll get a head start. Those guys at the roadblock don't have sightlines to the trail until we get up there a quarter mile."

"Just a minute," Lost Deer said. "Let me grab my rifle and that box of kitchen matches and the hatchet we kept from that last cabin." He also slung a canteen they had commandeered over his shoulder. It was three quarters full of water.

The pair moved quickly, crouched over as they ran into the fir and pine trees that bordered the parking lot of the lodge.

After getting the cabin number of the fugitives and warning the lodge manager to stay under cover, Yellowhenry and Whitedeer moved cautiously into position in front of cabin number four. With his Colt drawn and held in both hands in front of him, Yellowhenry yelled, "You in cabin number four! Come out with your hands up." He repeated the order twice more before looking at Whitedeer. "Stan, you give it a shot."

The bellow that rang from the lungs of the big man, made Shot Once and Lost Deer break into an involuntary sprint. "What the hell was that?" Shot Once asked when they had slowed to walking.

"Had to be Whitedeer. Sounded more like Big Foot, though. Having that sonofabitch on your trail wouldn't be too much different. Let's hustle," Lost Deer shivered.

"Give it one more shot, Stan," Yellowhenry said. He waited for the roar that emanated from the giant and echoed back off the ridges above the lake to cease.

"Joe, I think they're gone," Lost Deer said when the echoes had died away.

"All right. Cover me," Yellowhenry said as he approached the door. He turned the doorknob and shoved the door inside, stepping to the side. When nothing happened, he looked around the door frame. "Well, shit, Stan," he called. "They gave us the slip." The two officers looked at the stuff the escapees had left behind. A pair of holstered handguns and two sets of dirty clothes were the size of it.

"Why would they leave their pistols?" Whitehall asked.

"They're travelling light, and I'd guess they have heavier firepower that is more meaningful," Yellowhenry answered.

"So, they're on foot. They have to be headed for the Bob Marshall."

"I'd guess so. Here comes the blocking unit we called in. He must have seen something."

The partners stepped out to hear what the officer in the MHP cruiser had to say. "They're on the trail up the side," the patrolman reported. "Nearly half mile up, by now. I saw them running when that roar cut loose. What the hell was that, anyway?"

"Uh, this is Stan Whitedeer out of our Libby office. I'm Joe Yellowhenry from Havre."

"I'm Don Backstrom. Seeley Lake MHP. Jesus Christ, Stan. I've heard of you. Seven footer, I heard. Not to be rude, but you gotta be right at it, eh? Did you play a lot of basketball?"

Whitedeer didn't respond but when they shook hands, he exerted a little extra pressure, causing Backstrom to reach his hand behind his back where he flexed his fingers, making sure none were broken. His face washed white as he struggled to suck in the pain without showing it. "Say, I got a rifle. We might be able to pick 'em off when they cross clearings."

Yellowhenry had pulled a pair of binoculars from Whitedeer's rig. "So do they," he announced. "Scoped deer rifles. They're beyond a half mile. We'll rule that out."

"How the hell would prison escapees get rifles?" Backstrom asked.

"How would you do it in their shoes?" Yellowhenry asked.

"Steal 'em, I guess."

"There ya go. I'll bet they've been raiding vacant cabins."

"I'll be damned," the trooper said. "Has to be, don't it?"

"No doubt. You're going to be a busy boy for a couple of weeks documenting those break ins."

"Are you goin' after those guys?" Backstrom asked.

"Not really after them. We're going to push them over the top and into the Bob. Make them think there's no way for them to come back this way."

"Jesus Christ, you might as well kill 'em, then, if you get close enough. There's grizzlies all over that country. How would a man survive in there on foot?"

"Two reasons I can think of," Yellowhenry answered. "They have rifles, and they're Indians."

"Oh, yeah, I guess so," Backstrom said.

Whitedeer broke out in loud, guttural peals of laughter that made Yellowhenry smile wryly as he thought about having the big man trailing someone in the dark. He shuddered a little.

Chapter 11

Yellowhenry and Whitedeer followed cautiously. The trail switch backed so they were at times fairly close to the fleeing criminals. The trail also wound down side ridges and under rimrocks. Perfect echo chambers. Yellowhenry got an idea. "Hey, Stan," he asked, "how'd you like to have some fun?"

"What do you have in mind?"

"You yell, 'Henry, I'm comin' for ya!' It'll echo. As soon as the echo comes back, I'll yell, 'Kenny, I'm comin' for ya!'"

"Oh, yeah," Whitedeer grinned gleefully. "They'll shit their pants."

The intertwining shouts and echoes that blended and repeated were hair raising, even to the pair shouting them. The two escapees, at first, were puzzled by the overlay of the echoes until they picked out their names. "Kenny, do I hear your name?" Shot Once asked.

"Yeah, but if you listen to that growl, you'll hear 'Henry'," Lost Deer replied. "Then it's, 'I'm comin' for ya.' They're right down below us, but I can't see 'em."

"Should we hang up until we can get a shot and put 'em down."

"Hell, no. We'd have every branch of law enforcement plus half the military out here lookin' for us. If I go back to prison, it'll be for life, but at least it'll not be with a death sentence. If we get caught, or you do, Henry, they'll add ten years, maybe. You can survive that, but killin' lawmen will get you the needle sure as hell."

"Well, what are we carryin' these rifles for?"

"Bears, ya dumb shit. The Bob Marshall is a huge wilderness. There are Grizz in there that have never seen a man. We're gonna be meat on the hoof. They don't care if we walk upright or not."

"Why do I feel like I'm swan diving out of the frying pan?"

"Well, there's a chance you'll land on hot coals. Who knows? Maybe you're one of those guys who can run barefoot on coals."

For the next two hours the four men maintained their cat and mouse pursuit. A half hour before sundown, the prisoners broke over the crest and entered the wilderness. When they reached the top, the pursuing lawmen stood looking from the mountain crest in both directions. "Well, Yellowhenry," Whitedeer rumbled. "How long do you figure they'll last in there?"

"If they can find the horse trail coming up from the south, they can walk out in a week, or so," Yellowhenry answered. "If they're like most prisoners I know, one or both lacks the ability to cooperate for that long. I'd bet one or neither comes out."

"Yeah, I wouldn't second guess that. While we're still cooperatin', maybe we should head back down. Be dark in less than an hour."

"Lead the way," Yellowhenry laughed. "I don't want you runnin' over me in the dark."

Whitedeer chortled, "I might not recognize you as a bump in the road." Then they set off on the return to the Lodge at Holland Lake.

The lawmen spent the night at the lodge before returning to Deer Lodge. They reported to Aimes what they'd done, said 'so long', and returned to their home bases. By the time Yellowhenry returned home, he had been on the road for a total of six days. He had not checked into his office, partly due to the lack of cell service in the Swan Valley and partly because of a guilt complex arising from the near miss with Monti Collier. He had made it worse by stopping by for another cup of coffee at the Cascade Mountains Restaurant upon his return to Havre.

"Captain Joe!" Monti had squealed when she saw him seated on a stool at the breakfast counter. The restaurant, to his relief, was crowded. "Hey, everybody!" she called happily. "This is the famous Trooper Joe who said the Cascade is where you can get a perfect cup of Joe."

The place broke out in a round of applause that embarrassed the hell out of Yellowhenry. He was happy he was there for just a cup of coffee. Monti buzzed happily around him, even managing to smile with an implied promise and a lingering caress on his shoulder. He left shortly after, leaving a generous tip.

When he finally made it home, he was walking on eggshells. Amy, however, welcomed him warmly with a quick hug but no kiss. She let him check in with his children and smiled congenially as she served dinner. James gave him an update on things at school. "So, you aren't taking over as the classroom bully, are you?"

"No, but I sure have a lot of friends."

"Is there anything else you'd like to do, Son?"

"I'd like to take Judo again, Dad. I'll just learn the moves. I won't go after my sparring partners like I did before."

Yellowhenry ruffled James' hair. "I'll see what I can do, Son," he smiled.

He had finally relaxed and secretly thought everything was okay. He vowed never to risk temptation again. He was bracing for his pillow conversation with Amy. When she came from the bathroom, he was expecting her to be dressed in panties and a nightgown. She was wearing pajamas instead. Instead of lying down and cuddling, she sat cross-legged and stared at him.

"What?" he asked.

"Did you screw her?"

He looked at her and instantly knew. "No, Ames. I didn't."

"Does that mean, 'yet'?" she asked.

"No. But if you and I don't reestablish our equilibrium, who knows?" he said, his voice rising.

"You didn't report once to let me know what was happening, Joe. That makes me feel like 'equilibrium' is just some fancy idea you've made up."

"Well, it isn't. I don't care what you call it. Try 'balance' or 'understanding' or 'love', if that fits what you think we need. The Swan Valley has piss poor cell reception. There's a wide spot on a rise in the highway that announces cell reception. My work didn't pan out so I could tell the murderer I was chasing to, 'Hold on. I have to call my wife and report.'"

She looked at him carefully, looking for signs of duplicity. He looked steadily at her clearly leaving the ball in her court. "Okay," she said softly. "I don't have a word for it, Joe. But we aren't in this alone. We have six kids and a bun in the oven. Like it or not, if we don't do anything else, we're gonna fake it."

He looked at her and nodded. "Don't worry," he said. "You won't have to worry about faking anything in bed."

Chapter 12

Despite having just spent six days on the road, Yellowhenry, under the new aegis at home, took off on day trips. He drove out to Shelby for lunch at a restaurant that served a special sandwich. He stayed for most of the afternoon, drinking coffee and visiting with people who came in.

His third trip was to the east where he called on a lady rancher named Carolyn Malone, a widow with triplets. He spent an hour with her while her nanny entertained the youngsters. They had spent a platonic night in bed one time. Over the years, neither one had thought of it as more than a moment of kindness between friends. Her husband had just been killed by a grizzly bear and Yellowhenry had stayed at the ranch because of the late hour. It was she who had crawled into his bed.

After his third cup of coffee, Carolyn looked at him and grinned. "Joe," she said. "You want to take me for a tumble in the hay. I can tell."

He blushed, "What I want and what I'll do are two different things, Carolyn. But sure. I daydream a little about that night and how terrific you felt, pressed against my back. Your breasts, your pubic bone, your arm over my shoulder."

She giggled. "I shouldn't say this, but some of that was intentional. If you had just turned to your back, I would have had you. You were the perfect gentleman and faced away all night, stiff as a plank. You still are the perfect gentleman, Joe, but there's something wrong with you and Amy, isn't there?"

"How can you tell?"

"There's a certain sparkle to your eye and an intensity to your voice. I know when I'm being hustled, even if it's just for the thrill of possibilities. You've never done that before, honey."

"What?"

"Oops, I mean Joe," she laughed. "That just slipped out."

He chuckled, "We better not be caught at a dance where liquor is available. You wouldn't last till daylight."

"I wouldn't want to. Tell me, though, what's going on with you and Amy?"

"I can't put my finger on it, but how we relate has changed. We had a spat over something that involved the kids. It led to my leaving to pursue a case down south. I could have sent a deputy, but I took the assignment myself. For six days I was out of touch with my office and with Amy. When I got back, she all but accused me of having an affair."

"Did you?"

"No, but it was probably closer than the night you and I spent together."

"Was she hot?"

"Very, and also willing and ready. Joined me on a sofa wearing a see-through nightie. I admit I kissed her, but it was a goodbye kiss. I left before it could go any further."

"Don't tell me you told all that to Amy," Carolyn said, wide eyed.

"No, and I won't. She wanted to know if I'd screwed someone, though."

Carolyn laughed, "You men," she said. "You think you can sneak around and we wives won't know. It's so funny. Roy was like that. I actually felt sorry for him sometimes. He was such a good father and a good husband. He was just a man who needed five wives. How you don't get laid like a door mat is beyond me. Hell, I'd take you right now if you weren't such a good father and husband. My good friend, Amy, be damned."

He chuckled, "Reminds me of one time in high school. I had a girl all hot and ready, and all of a sudden she said, 'No. I can't do it, you're too nice.' I tried to convince her that it wasn't true, but she wouldn't do it."

"You are too nice, Joe. That's why you aren't a male whore. It's because you reject opportunity, nowadays, though. But if you ever change your mind, I have a hay loft ready at all times."

"Well," he chuckled, "I'll keep that in mind. I'd better be going."

When he stood up, she stepped into his arms and kissed him ardently. He returned the kiss in kind. She held his hand as she walked him out to his police cruiser. There, she kissed him again before turning and walking back to the house.

The relationship between Yellowhenry and his wife became more centered around their children and more detached from each other. While Amy could have provided conjugal privileges for another month, or so, she didn't. He took it upon himself to go to the hospital in Havre and arrange for a vasectomy. Amy did not get involved and took his week's leave from work matter of factly. At night, they were contented as they shared the trials and tribulations of their children. They accepted that their sex lives were on hold as Amy's pregnancy advanced. Often they slept with their one year old son, Waylon, who Amy would nurse to sleep. All three of them would get a good night's rest when she brought the baby to bed.

Charlie Goodwoman continued to come to town bi-monthly for food and supplies to run his business. When he showed up at the highway patrol office, and Yellowhenry wasn't there, he would load up his purchases and drive out to the reservation. Minnie would invite him in for his shower, but she had gone to a secondhand store in Havre and bought him an extra pair of pants and a shirt. At first, he had protested that she was spoiling all his fun, but she told him it was her way or the highway. As a result, he stopped his nude romping around her house. "Hell, Minnie," he admitted. "I was just pretending to be a sex maniac."

"Good," she told him. "I wasn't pretending to make a shorthorn out of you if you didn't stop."

As a result, the two of them struck up a different kind of relationship. Charlie had found a market for canned and dried snake meat. His first harvest came from the wild ones. Then, his pregnant females provided young that Charlie fed baby mice. After they had shed their skins twice, he jarred them up and sold them to his supplier, the same outlet that bought his snake venom. The meat went to Chinatown in San Francisco.

So, with time on his hands when he came to town, Charlie started hunting rattlers in the bottom of the draw beyond Yellowhenry's horse pasture. Minnie joined him. He gave her a set of snake tongs while he used a hook and his hands.

The small stream that wended its way supported willows, cottonwoods, brush, weeds, and grass. It was perfect habitat for squirrels, rats, and mice. The snakes followed.

In their chasing the snakes, the pair found that, often, instead of standing their ground and rattling, the snakes would take off and crawl into rock crevices and rodent holes.

Charlie was quite adept at grabbing a retreating snake and pulling it free while swinging it out at arm's length until he could get it into clear ground where he would drop it up and down until it crawled away rather than at him when it touched down. Then he would pin its head with his hook long enough to grab it behind the head with his left hand. He carried a five gallon bucket with a double lid he had specially developed. A third of the way down, a specially weighted pivot lid would swing down, dropping the captured snakes into the bottom of the bucket. Minnie's job, when he had the snake in hand, was to hold the top lid, which was fitted with a pair of metal handholds set in opposition and a couple of inches inside the rim. She would quickly slap it over the snake when Charlie had it positioned so he could throw the snake onto the closed inner lid. The swing lid would be pulled down by the weight of the snake into the bottom. Then, the lid would swing back up, opening the upper chamber for the next snake.

The most exciting time was Minnie's slapping the top lid quickly enough to keep the muscular, twisting, and angry serpent inside the smaller compartment. It thrilled her to make a neat capture, but the excitement of the operation was when a snake was only partially trapped in the upper chamber. Minnie had to judge the capture and decide whether to turn the snake loose for recapture or to manipulate her lid to hold it well enough so that Charlie could use his hook to stuff the serpent into the bucket. The key was to track the head. With it constrained, the body could usually be manipulated to drop it where they wanted.

Chapter 13

When Yellowhenry found out, he marched directly to Minnie's house and demanded to know what the hell she thought she was doing. "Working," she said calmly. "I'm getting paid to catch snakes."

"Do you know how dangerous it is to handle rattlesnakes?" he asked, his voice strained to keep from shouting.

"Of course. I wouldn't think of working with you."

"But you're good with a man who chases you naked around your house?"

"Of course not. I bought him extra clothes so when he gets out of the shower, he can get dressed. So, he quit chasin' and we went huntin' snakes."

"Minnie, it's still too dangerous."

"Would you call Charlie an expert?"

"Well, yes. But you could still get bitten."

She looked at him oddly with her head held at an angle. "Hmmm," she expressed.

"What does that mean?"

"You have six kids on the ground and one coming in on approach. Do you really need another one?"

"I'm not trying to make you one of my kids, Minnie."

"You could have fooled me. So, now that that's all settled, why don't you come along and see how we do it? That way you can quit pretending that I need a father."

"I'm not pretending you need a father. I'm concerned for your safety."

"Are you firing me?"

"Don't make this petty, Minnie."

"I'm handling rattlers, Joe, as a partner with an expert snake handler who has a good market for their meat. We're making good money, not that that is any more of your business than your telling me I have no right to wrangle snakes. So, butt out."

"If you're doing this for meat, why don't you shoot them?"

"Charlie milks them for venom, first."

"You're not calling it quits, are you?"

"As your mother? No, I'm not."

"All right," he laughed. "When do we go snake huntin'."

Goodwoman came into town a few days later and called on Yellowhenry at his patrol office. "Well, Charlie, you are full of surprises, aren't you?"

He cackled and looked at Yellowhenry in amusement. "Don't tell me you are missing some snakes down in your bottom property. Minnie and I haven't caught a single one with a brand."

"Well, today, I'm gonna be the brand inspector, Charlie. Minnie has given me a special invitation."

"Well, Joe," Charlie grinned, "from my personal observation, your snake handling skills are a bit heavy handed."

"They haven't improved much, Charlie. But tell me about your partnership with Minnie. What's her cut?"

"After expenses, we put the money in our joint account."

"You don't split it down the middle? Your share and her share?"

"No. We both have access to all the money."

"How much money are you talking about, Charlie?"

"I'm not sure. I don't pay much attention. Last time I looked at a statement a couple months ago, it was about a hundred thousand."

"You and Minnie have made that much?" Yellowhenry gulped.

"No. I had some in there before we started. Minnie and I have tossed in a few thousand."

"Wait a minute. Minnie is signed onto the money you had before you teamed up?"

"Why not? We're partners. We're taking care of each other. She's been out learning the rest of the business. She's the one who cans the meat. She milks good, too."

"Yeah? Well, no shit, Charlie. You fooled me. I had no idea Minnie has so many hidden talents."

Chapter 14

Henry Shot Once and Kenny Lost Deer pressed on into the Bob Marshall Wilderness without pausing until they were certain that the lawmen who had pursued them to the crest of the mountain had stopped.

"Well," Shot Once said, "let's drag out our Indian skills and figure out how we're gonna get through tonight."

Lost Deer looked at his partner and made a quick assessment of what he could expect. He wasn't much impressed. He looked around in a 360 degree sweep.

"What are you looking for?" Shot Once asked.

"Downed tree where we can shelter in the cavity of the root ball."

"Yeah, good idea," Shot Once agreed. "See anything?"

"Nothing here. Look for something where trees fall downslope. They'll tear out a bigger hole."

The men spent fifteen minutes hurrying from sightline to sightline before they found a suitable fallen tree that had pulled up enough of a root ball that the hollow was adequate for them to stretch out without lying on top of each other. "If you want to gather some wood for a fire," Lost Deer said, "I'll work on clearing out the cavity and building a bed platform."

"What's wrong with it as it is?"

"It isn't level. It's too small for the two of us unless we sit up all night. Is that what you want to do?"

"Not really, I guess."

"I'll help gather wood when I'm finished. Gonna be cold tonight. Fire is crucial."

Shot Once looked around and began a listless campaign that showed no promise of producing what they would need to maintain a small warming fire. Lost Deer used the hatchet to chop roots and hack dirt. He worked feverishly as light faded. His assessment of Shot Once was proving to be accurate when he looked up to see the man squatting down watching him work. Not really satisfied, Lost Deer decided to make do with what he had. Then, he moved quickly to a pair of fir trees with low hanging branches and chopped off boughs until he had a double arm load. He carried them to the cavity and spread them out as a one man bed. Shot Once asked, "We gonna sleep in each other's arms, or what?"

Lost Deer tossed him the hatchet. "Go cut your own. I'm gonna gather firewood."

"I've done that," Shot Once said.

"It's a good start, but we'll need more than that. Hurry up if you want boughs for your bed. I could use the hatchet getting wood."

"Take it. I don't mind a little dirt where I sleep."

Lost Deer worked, chopping dead branches until it was too dark to see. Shot Once watched, not making a move to help until Lost Deer shouted, "Come drag branches, Henry. You're gonna need fire as much as I am."

With Lost Deer showing anger and impatience, Shot Once began helping. Their wood pile was not what Lost Deer wanted. He decided to build three kindling and burn piles so that they could rebuild the fire twice during the night. "What the hell," Shot Once said. "Aren't we gonna keep the fire burning all night."

"We don't have that much wood, Henry. The coldest part will be toward morning. We're gonna have to be cold some of the time. We'll restart the fire and warm up as we need to. If we're careful, three fires should last four, maybe five hours. Right now, we don't need a fire. I'll build one as soon as it gets cold enough that we begin to shiver. Couple of hours from now."

"How about we each build a fire when we're ready and use the third fire for the cold of the morning?"

"No. I'll take care of the fire."

"What makes you so damned high and mighty?" Shot Once demanded.

"I have the matches. Now let's get some rest while it's still warm."

"I need some water," Shot once said.

Lost Deer handed him the canteen. He drank deeply and then hung the canteen around his neck.

"What are you doing?" Lost Deer asked.

"You have the matches, I have the water."

A moment later, Lost Deer's rifle boomed and dirt showered down on Shot Once. He squalled and fell to his side, "What are you shootin' for?" he cried.

"Give me the canteen," Lost Deer said calmly racking another shell into his rifle's barrel, "or the next one won't be so pleasant."

"All right," a thoroughly alarmed Shot Once said. "Jesus Christ, you don't have to go off the deep end about it." He handed over the canteen. Lost Deer took a modest drink and tucked the canteen into a depression in the backwall of the cavity on his side of the sleep hole. He stretched out on his bough bed with his rifle beside him set on safety but with the barrel pointed at Shot Once.

The night went as Lost Deer thought, except that he woke to find Shot Once tossing wood from the second fire pile onto the first fire. "So, you plan to burn the wood till it's gone?" he asked.

"I'm cold. You said if we got cold, we'd start a fire," Shot Once shrugged and tossed another branch onto the fire.

"All right, Henry, have it your way," Lost Deer said.

"Aren't you gonna argue about it?"

"Nope. I'm gonna go to sleep and let you burn up the wood."

Shot Once looked at his companion suspiciously, wondering what was going on in the man's head. "I'm gonna keep an eye on you, by god," he muttered. "Sneaky son of a bitch. Got a plan you ain't sharin'. I'd bet my entire wad on it."

Shot Once ran through the last of the wood at around two o'clock in the morning. Lost Deer had slept long and hard by all appearances. Shot Once would build fire, nod off, build fire, and nod off again. The morning chill woke him after the fire had gone cold and there was so more wood. He looked around and was shocked to find Lost Deer's bed empty. "Hey, Kenney!" he shouted in alarm. "You out takin' a piss?"

Then, he noticed that Lost Deer's rifle, the camp hatchet, and the water canteen were missing. His wail of despair was long and loud. Lost Deer, who was a half mile away heard it and ignored it. He was on the trail leading downhill. Making headway wasn't easy, but it was keeping him warm.

Chapter 15

Yellowhenry had to admit that Goodwoman and Minnie were an accomplished and smooth working team. They were both wearing knee high snake boots and they kept their hands and arms clear of areas where a snake could strike them. Once in a while, Charlie would grab a retreating rattler and handle it with his bare right hand, but Minnie never did. She used her snake tongs to grab snakes which she handed off to Charlie.

In addition to their capture bucket, they brought along a pair of five gallon storage buckets. They hunted for three hours and called it off with ten snakes captured. Yellowhenry was impressed. "You two are really slick," he said. "My compliments to you, Charlie, and I'll not say another word to Minnie about this being too dangerous for her to get involved in."

"That's good," Minnie grinned, "but you ain't done. This is only half the work. You're comin' out to Greasewood Junction to see how we do the rest of it."

"I've been out there, Minnie. I have nightmares about it."

"Well, what did you expect?" Goodwoman asked indignantly. "You had me jailed for four days. My place doesn't run itself. It takes management."

"Yeah, it does. But I didn't jail you. I got you released on your own recognizance. You were just lucky you didn't go to jail for about five years for throwing that snake on that schoolteacher."

"Not my brightest moment," Goodwoman agreed. "When I say 'you', I mean the law in general. I thank you for helping me out."

"How did all that sort out for you, anyway?"

"My jail time was reduced to time served, and I had to pay a thousand dollar fine, plus they reduced my operator's license to probationary status. I have to operate for three years with no other incidents like that. I am banned from presenting in schools. I definitely got the shitty end of the deal."

"Well, it's a damned good thing you didn't toss one at me," Yellowhenry said. "You, that snake, and your entire operation would be toes up."

"I'm stupid, Joe, but I ain't crazy."

"Ha!" Minnine snorted. "That's still up for debate."

"Is your civil suit settled?" Yellowhenry asked.

"I pled poverty. We settled for monthly payments. I have to shell out a hundred a month until I've paid that prick $15,000. I can pay it all off at one time if I get a little money ahead."

"How did you hide the hundred grand you told me about?"

"It wasn't in my name for a while. Simple."

"Well, all righty, then. Let's go see the other half of this wrangle."

Yellowhenry drove separately with Minnie by his side. "How did you get him to sign you onto his bank account, Minnie?" Yellowhenry asked on the way out.

"Before I bought him that change of clothes, I slowed down a little three or four times."

"Well, okay. That's a question I'd rather not have asked."

"I'll never use any of his money, Joe. I just took over bookkeeping for both of us. I know what my share is. I've done a little research on the computers at the community center, and made some price adjustments to our product line. His distributor wasn't worth a damn, so I lined him up with a new one. He moves three times the volume and pays us on time. Our prices are better. He even places orders so we know how to package the product. It's just better all the way around."

"Well, I still worry about snakebite, Minnie. Not just to you, but to Charlie as well."

"I've had to kick him in the ass, Joe, about that. He gets too damned comfortable with snakes he calls his pets. Now that we've got steady, even growing, demand, I make him pay attention to process. He's really much better than when I first started helping him."

"Wow, I'm impressed and pleased. How many milkers does he have now?"

"It isn't how many there are like in a dairy. Snakes can only be milked once every sixty days. It takes a lot of snake power to milk a snake a day. We don't have a big enough complex for that. Sixty milkers that would have to be fed, watered, cleaned up after, helped with their shedding. Kept warm and protected. We're milking three snakes a week. Takes thirty that have to be catalogued so they don't get milked too often. And the mice! We feed the little snakes twice a week. The bigger ones every seven days. That's a lot of mice."

"How often are you going out there, Minnie?"

"Half a day three days a week. Charlie comes and gets me. I do the paperwork from home."

He reached across and pressed her hand. "I'm proud of you, Minnie."

She curled her fingers in his and they held hands. They finished the trip like a pair of teenagers. He was surprised from their chatter to learn that she and Goodwoman were discussing a permanent relationship. "You're thinking marriage, Minnie?" he asked.

"No. Business. There is a real demand for our snake products. We're thinking about expansion."

"Are you going to move out here?"

"Only temporarily. Of course, he won't be moving in with me. Can you imagine all those snakes in town?"

"I can't. But I can't imagine you not living in your place either.

"Well, I'm not going to do that. We're looking for a trainee."

"That could be a long search," he said.

"Well, not too long," she grinned, snuggling against him.

"Why do I feel like I'm going to be creeped out?"

"James wants to learn the business."

"James!" he exclaimed.

"He says he needs a summer job. If he is serious, he needs some training."

"Have you run this by Amy?"

"Sure. She's good with it. Had to promise, he would not handle snakes. He'll take care of mice and clean cages. We had to buy him snake boots first."

"I see," he said dourly. "You need to show me today exactly what James will be doing. Rest assured, I'll monitor all summer long what he does, too."

"We wouldn't want it any other way, Joe," Minnie said.

"Oh, I wouldn't either, Minnie. I wouldn't want to disappoint James," he said. "Since his Judo lessons, he's really blossomed."

"You and I are still on the same dock," she returned. "We still have some boats out to sea though."

"You're referring to Amy, now. Hopefully, her boat won't sink," he said, suddenly sober.

"A word to the wise," Minnie said looking closely at Yellowhenry. "Keep your dock in good repair, so her boat has a place to tie up to when it does come back from the sea."

Chapter 16

Kenney Lost Deer was beginning to move much more quickly as daylight began to brighten the gloom of the shallow side canyon he had turned down into. He was beginning to process the possibility of being a captive of the Bob Marshall Wilderness for a long time. As a result, he dusted off his survival skills. His thoughts turned to how his ancestors lived happily in such places. He took inventory of what he had and what he would need from the Bob Marshall Wilderness.

The side canyon was running a small stream of water below the geme trail that ran parallel to the watercourse some thirty yards above. Lost Deer slowed and began stalking. Twenty minutes later he was set up on a dry mule deer doe as she sucked water from the stream. The range was sharply downhill and seventy yards. He toyed with the idea of taking the head shot, but he was uncertain of where the rifle he was carrying was sighted in. So, he moved the crosshairs on the bottom line of the doe behind the point of the shoulder. At the sound of the shot, the doe bucked, spun, and sprinted back up the sidehill for thirty yards before piling up in buckbrush.

Lost Deer had completed gutting the doe and had laid the edible organs out to the side when he heard Henry Shot Once shouting from the other side of the drainage. "Hey, Kenney!" the man's yells rang out. "Where the hell are you?"

Lost Deer wiped his clasp knife's blade on his pants and sat back on his haunches. He didn't answer Shot Once's shouts. A half hour later, the man came chugging up from the stream. When he was ten yards away he looked up and stopped. Lost Deer was standing with his rifle akimbo beside a screen of timber into which he could quickly step and take cover. The men eyed each other for a few moments, neither saying anything. Finally, Lost Deer walked forward, "Are you here to fight?" he asked.

"No. That would be foolish," Shot Once answered.

"What is it you want?"

"We need to team up."

"Your idea of teaming up makes me work twice as hard as you do. No thanks."

"I will be equal."

"When you aren't, I'll shoot you."

"Working together, we can survive this. Alone, we might not."

"I know that, but after your performance last night, I'd be better off alone."

"I get it, Kenney. We both have to pull our own weight. I will pull mine from here on out."

"You'd better start thinking like an Indian, then. Not like a white man."

"All right. Let's process this deer."

The pair, finally working together equally, dragged the doe carcass uphill fifty yards to a narrow bench where they could work, skinning and boning the kill. As they worked they talked and schemed about how they were to survive. "After last night," Shot Once said, "we've got to find shelter of some kind besides the cavities of root balls."

"Up toward the top there should be caves," Lost Deer said. "I wouldn't be surprised if we found some the ancients used."

"What do you have in mind for all this meat?" Shot Once asked.

"If we can figure out how to split it up, with hide, organs and boned out meat, we'll each have about sixty pounds to pack."

"What if we split the hide and make a poke of however much we can carry in a poke? Might not be all of it, but there's more than enough to carry us over to another kill," Shot Once offered.

Lost Deer looked at the mound of meat they'd placed on the hide. "Yeah, I see what you mean. I'm for leaving the organs except for maybe one serving for variety. What do you think?"

"I don't eat liver or heart. So, I'll leave that up to you."

"I like a slice of liver now and then. All right, I'll cut enough liver to roast tonight. The scavengers can have the rest of it. Are you carrying a pocketknife?"

"I always have my multi-tool," Shot Once replied. "It's a skinny kind of Leatherman, but it carries a five inch blade. What's on your mind?"

"That hide is big enough that we could both have a vest. To tan it, we'll need to make a brain paste with fat. I'll use the hatchet to crack the skull of this deer, and while I spread it apart, you can cut out as much brain as you can."

"Do you know how to tan a hide?" Shot Once asked. "I don't."

"I do. It's a lot of damned work, but having a waterproof and warm vest will be a big payoff."

"Show me what to do, and I'll get on it," Shot Once said.

"Good," Lost Deer grinned. "I'll work on mine, and you'll work on yours."

With each doing his equal share, by late afternoon they were at the base of a long rimrock about a third of the way down from the crest of the Swan Mountain Range which bordered the wilderness. They were deciding on which of three caves that were large enough for them to move into. Shot Once liked one with a crawl-in entrance that, after fifteen feet, opened up into a cavern with a ten foot ceiling and twenty by thirty foot floor. An open gash in the roof let in enough light to see without the need of torches.

Lost Deer looked on it as a one-way trap. "If you like it Henry, have at it," he said. "I'm going to move into this one." He walked twenty paces along the ledge fronting the line of a dozen smaller caves of various depths and dimensions. The opening required him to stoop to enter, but it opened up right away to a cavern with a twelve foot roof and a fifteen by twenty-five foot floor that tapered back into a deeper recess that he hadn't explored.

What he particularly liked was that the opening was overtopped by a narrow wedge shaped crack which provided light and drew dust outward when he tossed dirt into the air. He also noticed that the floor toward the cave mouth was charred. He grinned, and whispered, "Grandfather, you were here."

When the pair rejoined a few minutes later, Lost Deer was already tossing rocks for a fire ring toward the entrance to his cave. Shot Once came crawling on his hand and knees from the tunnel leading into the cave he had chosen. "Kenney," he said immediately. "Is there room for both of us in your cave? This one is ridiculous now that I've crawled into and out of it."

"Of course. It is accustomed to many occupants."

"What? Down here?" Shot Once asked. "There's nobody in this whole damned wilderness but us."

"Used to be," Lost Deer said. "But thousands of years ago, before the Europeans, our people were nomadic out on the plains for hundreds, maybe thousands of years, and had no use for this place. But before the nomads, we had ancestors who did. Their fires left their mark on the floor. I'll bet deeper inside we find their paintings on the walls, too."

"What do you want to bet we find graffiti, too?" Shot Once hooted.

"Good one, Henry," Lost Deer chuckled. "There better not be. This is a sacred place."

"Jesus, Kenney," Shot Once said soberly, "after all, it's just a cave."

"Yes. But we are going to treat it like the Sistine Chapel, Henry, or you'd be wise to make yourself a pair of knee pads to use as you crawl into and out of your cave."

"All right, I get it. I admit I have never been into ancient history and all that. But if it means all that to you, I'll respect it, too."

"You'd better."

Chapter 17

It was midsummer when Yellowhenry and his sergeant Art McClintock caught a weird one. A herd of five Indian horses were reported wandering aimlessly along the highway heading out toward Shelby. When a horse had stumbled out of the dark in front of an eighteen wheeler, the driver had blasted his air horn, swerved to avoid the collision, and shifted his load, causing him to have to stop in Havre and work for eight hours resetting the cargo.

When he finished the work, the pissed off driver decided to let the reservation police know that the goddamned Indians needed to keep their goddamned ponies off the goddamned highway. His diatribe was fielded by Officer Cold Hawk. He was a man of some seventy years who had taken his assignment at the front desk of police headquarters very seriously. At one time, he had even been on the force. "Where were the goddamned Indian horses that were on the goddamned highway goddamned at?" he asked seriously.

"Are you trying to be a smartass?" the driver demanded.

"Not a goddamned bit more than you are," Cold Hawk said calmly.

"They were out toward Shelby. Maybe twenty miles. Goddamnit!," the driver shouted. "I could have been killed."

"That's too goddamned bad," Cold Hawk said. "Tell me, for my report, how fast you were driving at the time."

"Out in the middle of nowhere, seventy, or so. Certainly less than eighty."

"That goddamned country out there is goddamned open range, sir. If you'd killed one of those goddamned Indian horses, you would have been responsible for paying the tribe the value of the animal. And you know what? The tribe doesn't have a horse on the highway worth less than $2,500. You were goddamned lucky, sir. Oh, and by the way. The goddamned speed limit in this goddamned state is fifty-five at night. Could I get your name and the name of the company you drive for? This call has been recorded. Just so you know."

"To hell with you!" the man shouted. "This has been a goddamned waste of my time." He disconnected the call.

"Well," Cold Hawk said. "I'll be goddamned." Then he called and reported the driver's report to Yellowhenry.

"There shouldn't be any Indian horses out that way, Art," Yellowhenry said, sharing the information. "That's ranching country, but that's quite a ways from the reservation. We need to get out there and round up those horses before someone is hurt."

"We'll have to rent a truck and trailer. Do you want to be in on it?"

"Do we have any other cowboys on staff with a handy horse?"

"Just Zane Hammond, but he's out on patrol to the east."

"Looks like you and me, Art."

The sergeant, who was a man in his early fifties was the possessor of a deeply seamed and craggy face that looked decidedly simian. He gazed at his boss through one blue eye and one brown eye and flapped his gigantic ears in an elephantine imitation.

Although he had seen the demonstration many times, Yellowhenry couldn't help but laugh uproariously. "Damn you, Art. You get me every time you do that. You go get the truck and trailer and pick me up at my place in an hour. I'll have my horse saddled and ready to load."

When McClintock pulled into the yard at Yellowhenry's reservation home, the captain's horse, a sorrel gelding he called Hi Boy was saddled and ready to go. There was also a fifteen gallon galvanized tub and four sealed five gallon jerry cans set out to load, as well.

"What's with the gas cans, Joe?" McClintock asked.

"They're water cans, Art. I have a feeling that those horses out there could be dehydrated and that could be adding to their behavior."

"Could be," the big man said as he grabbed a pair of the cans and walked them to the rear of the eight horse trailer he'd rented.

They finished loading and were about to pull out, when Amy called from the back door of the house. "Joe," she said. "Take this with you. In case you get delayed."

"What is it?" he asked.

"A thermos of coffee and some sandwiches for you and Art. There's an extra cup in the box."

"Thank you, honey," Yellowhenry smiled in appreciation.

McClintock leaned forward from the passenger's side, caught Amy's eye, flapped his ears, and said, "Yes, honey, thank you very much."

Amy burst into laughter. She was still laughing when she returned to the house as the men pulled away.

Chapter 18

"What the hell?" Charlie Goodwoman puzzled when he went to check on his venom horses. All five were missing. He walked the fence line and found the problem. From the tracks he could see where all five had run from one side of the enclosure to the other and through the one strand wire fence. "Goddamnit," he muttered. "Something spooked them to make them ignore the plastic strips and the wire."

He had fenced in seven acres for the five horses he had bought from the reservation. That he owned only five of the fenced acres was an annoyance he'd deal with later, if necessary. Being in a hurry, he had hired a couple of men to put up an electrified one strand fence with plastic strips attached to provide a visual barrier.

The impetus for acquiring horses was the lucrative market provided by the immunity of horse serum used in the production of antivenin for rattlesnake bites. Minnie had explained it all to him and they had gone through all the steps of upgrading his license to use horses in the production of the serum. The promise of fat profits had jump-started his injection of the horses with snake venom. That he had overdone it was apparent when he found he'd killed one of his original horses. He'd replaced the horse and roughly followed the given guidelines for the injection process. Nevertheless, the horses were often queasy for a few days.

Minnie gave him hell when he had to admit the horses were gone. "I told you that fence needed to be upgraded, damnit!" she shouted. "But you knew better, just like you always think you do. Now, what are you gonna do, Charlie?"

"Go buy some more horses, I guess."

"Oh, no you don't," she said angrily. "You are gonna hire a couple of Indian wranglers to round up those we have. I'm gonna contract a crew to put up a proper fence."

"Well, we won't make any money for quite a while is all I have to say."

"If you'd dragged that horse you killed out where I told you to, you wouldn't have had that bear, or whatever it was, spooking those horses. You keep up your bullshit, 'I know best,' approach and you'll lose your license to do anything with snakes, Charlie."

"I'll always have my snakes, Minnie," he said stubbornly.

"Yeah, you will," she retorted, "until the law takes them away from you and throws your ass in jail. Don't forget, it's on your record that you threw a fully envenomated snake onto that schoolteacher."

"Damned teacher had it comin'," he growled.

"For a hundred dollars, Charlie?" she said in disbelief. "That attitude of yours is why we're having this conversation. It makes you stupidly dangerous, and you aren't stupid. So, knock it off. Go find some people who can get our horses back."

She turned on her heel and stalked back to the improved clinic which contained her private office. Her influence on the operation was apparent in the improvements that had been made since she'd made her appearance. A second story containing an apartment had been added to the original structure, and a long lean-to added off to the east side, more than doubled the workspace Charlie had before her arrival. A well had been drilled so that running water could be piped into the facility, and a power line had been run in from the main line at the highway,

The overall appearance and functional capability was profound. From the shack of a queer snake handler to a facility that was a primary producer of snake products, both for consumption and for medical purposes was astounding.

Yellowhenry and McClintock were driving slowly in the area indicated by the truck driver, but there were no horses in sight and they hadn't discovered pony tracks, either. After touring a ten mile stretch back and forth three times, Yellowhenry looked at his partner and said, "What the hell, Art? What do you say we drive out to Shelby for lunch and take another look this afternoon?"

"Sounds good to me. I'm slavering for one of those tuna sandwiches from Addy's Drive in."

"Let's keep our ears open while we're there," Yellowhenry said. "Maybe someone else saw those horses."

Minnie checked the balance in their joint account. Despite the expense so far accrued in the site's upgrade, there was still a touch over a hundred thousand dollars. She had added twenty-five thousand of her own, so she felt justified in ordering up a new fence to enclose forty acres, a hay barn, and a stable. The fifty thousand dollar project was aimed at the inclement weather of winter and spring. She knew how two horses could tromp and defecate a five acre enclosure into a hock deep, reeking mud pit. That five would serve to deepen the mess into a belly deep mire was absolutely certain. That could be largely avoided by fencing in forty acres. Her contract called for a concrete floor in the barn and stable. "Charlie's gonna crap a blue bean when he sees this," she muttered.

Chapter 19

Kenney Lost Deer and Henry Shot Once, having set up a living space in the main cavern of their cave, had put together torches of pine branches smeared with pitch and deer fat. A few days later, they were looking in awe at cave paintings in a deeper recess of the tube that terminated in a ballroom sized cavern with a smooth sheer face on the mountain side. It had been painted by a civilization long lost. "Jesus, Kenney," Henry exclaimed, his voice reverberating in the chamber. "That's a fuckin' elephant right there."

"Mammoth, Henry. That's a mammoth. They disappeared from this country ten, maybe twelve thousand years ago. Our people were here. The Ancients. This is a holy place."

The men stared at the drawings. One of particular note was of an Irish Elk. "That means our people travelled," Kenney explained. "The Irish Elk disappeared a couple thousand years ago. It was an animal of Europe and Asia. Its image is here because our people came from there. The other animals, buffalo, elk, deer, antelope, rabbits, and wolves are all from here."

"Are we gonna add to it?" Henry asked.

"Are you naturally stupid, or did you have to work at it, Henry?" Lost Deer asked.

"Hey, you don't need to get personal about it. I was just askin' is all."

"Would you go to the Sistine Chapel and add a little?"

"Well, no a' course not. That's a recognized sacred site."

"This would be, too," Kenney said. "Think of it. We are maybe the only two who have been in here for thousands of years. This documents our people's presence clear back before the end of the last ice age. That is incredible, Henry. Don't you feel a sense of awe?"

"I s'pose so. I'd still like to add our initials, real small. I mean, if they did a whole wall, what would our adding our initials matter. No one will ever be in here as long as the federal government is in charge."

"Do you like graffiti, Henry?"

"Some of it."

"Well, it doesn't belong here. That's what your initials in here would be. Knock yourself out in the first cavern, but leave this alone. You touch this and I'll kill ya."

"All right, goddamnit. You're a real touchy son of a bitch sometimes. Do you know that?" Henry said as he turned to leave. Lost Deer followed him out.

"You're a real lost cause, Henry. One that might not make it back to civilization," he muttered under his breath.

Yellowhenry and McClintock were listening to an irate westbound motorist who had seen the horses just before sunrise. "Someone is responsible for those damned horses," the wife of the husband was saying loudly. "If we hadn't been going seventy, we woulda plowed right into them. As it was we dodged them. It was a miracle we weren't killed."

"Why don't you talk to those two fellas sitting right over there," the waitress offered. "They're highway patrolmen. Maybe they can shed some light on it."

The woman looked at the pair of cowboy like officers who looked directly at her. "What about it?" she asked loudly. "Why are you sitting in here with those horses out there on the highway?"

"Tell her, Art," Yellowhenry said. "I look like one of those Injins who wouldn't know jack about anything."

"Okay," McClintock grinned. "I promise I won't flap my ears." He stood up and strolled to the booth across the restaurant where the man and woman were seated on opposite sides of a booth. He pulled a chair from a table and set it so he could sit at their booth. They drew back into the booth, he defensively, and she offensively, as they shifted their food between them and him. "I'm Art McClintock, Montana Highway Patrol Sergeant assigned to the Havre office. Who are you folks?"

"I'm Chris Coyne," the whipped middle aged husband said. "This is my wife, Stella."

"My pleasure, I'm sure," McClintock said, shaking hands with both. "So, was it still dark when you passed those horses?"

"So what if it was?" the woman asked belligerently. "What does that have to do with it?"

"I take it you folks are not from ranching country, so when you passed those signs that said 'Open Range' they probably didn't register. Is that about right?"

"They could have said 'Closed Range'. Are we supposed to know what that would mean, too?" Stella demanded more than asked. She was a plump dishwater blonde with a round face and pug nose, along with a small mouth with bright red lipstick smeared by the burger she was eating. Her eyes were without shadow or color, lending their all black color to give her a rather porcine appearance.

"Well, there you go," Art smiled. "What they mean is that the roads aren't fenced to keep livestock off the roads and rights of way. So, if you kill or injure livestock that's on the road in an area that is designated Open Range, you are responsible to the owner of the animal for its value."

"Well, that's a pile of crap," she said angrily. "Who is responsible if we get killed because we ran into someone's horse out on the highway?"

"Did you see the speed limit signs that said, '55 at night'? I guess I should ask you, Chris," Art said amiably, ignoring her outburst.

"Well, yeah, I suppose so, but it's a road that goes straight as a string for miles at a time. I pressed it a little bit, I suppose. I certainly wasn't the only one."

"I don't doubt it a bit," Art chuckled. "But I must tell you that at 55 mph, you have a much better chance of not overdriving your headlights which eliminates your stopping distance. I'd hate to see you folks hurt out in open country. Sometimes you don't even get cell phone reception out there. Even if someone came along, getting an ambulance to you could be a matter of hours. That makes an accident a life and death matter more often than I care to remember."

"Now, I suppose you're going to tell us that someone is killed out there three times a week because they drove faster than 55 at night," Stella said, rolling her eyes.

"Oh, no, not at all," Art said quietly. "But when you are the one responsible for pulling someone from a burning car as they scream while their intestines spill through your hands onto the highway, you never want to experience anything close to it again."

She looked at him to see if he was being hyperbolic to make a point, but when he looked at her kindly before turning to her husband, she slowly closed her mouth cutting off her next comment. Art stood and shook Coyne's hand, saying, "I hope this explanation helps a little bit. It's been a pleasure speaking to you folks. Have a nice rest of your trip. Ma'am," he said with a tip of his hat as he looked at her politely.

When he reset the chair to the table he'd pulled it from, he heard the man hiss at his wife, "Not one more word from you, Stella. That man is an example of what real professional lawmen should be like everywhere. Just shut your big mouth."

Chapter 20

Minnie was facing off with Charlie. "I've never wanted to be a goddamned corporation, for Chrissakes, Minnie. Look at how big this has gotten?"

"That is an accusation against me. So, let me lay it out for you. When I came out here, you were already past just milking snakes. So, I optimized the operation. Made it more efficient and more profitable. Getting horses was your idea. What you neatly overlooked is what happens in wet weather when penned up animals can't get out of their shit and piss infused mud hole. They have to sleep in it and pick their feed from it. It's cruelty to animals, Charlie. I won't have it. Now, I've pitched in twenty-five thousand of my own dollars to put up a decent barn and stable, and a fence to give those horses room to survive decently when we're three feet deep in snow or a foot deep in mud.

"If that overwhelms you, because now you work in a first class clinic instead of a shack barely better than your outhouse, Charlie, I'll turn the books over to you, cancel the construction contract and get back what I can of my twenty-five thousand, and say goodbye."

"Damnit Minnie," Charlie said. "I know I do the same stuff on a bigger scale but look at this place. I'm just sort of overwhelmed. I mean who would believe I'd ever be in charge of something like this?"

"Well, here's an idea for you. James is developing more than a passing interest. Groom him to help you and as he gets older, you can turn it over to him and you can become the assistant. That will make you happy in your own mind. You can finish where you believe you belong. On the bottom looking up."

"You make all that seem so empty in value, Minnie. Like I'm a hollow man."

"Then find a way to fill yourself, Charlie. Maybe by helping James fill himself."

Yellowhenry and McClintock found the horses on their way back to Havre. By the time they were located, none were queasy, but all were easily haltered as they crowded the tub to drink water. "Never saw horses drier than those," McClintock said.

"Not sure I have either," Yellowhenry said. "Where the hell they came from and who owns them is the next part of this puzzle. For now, let's take them to my place."

With the horses turned into the lower pasture, they developed a habit of coming up to water at the stable corral and then returning. As a result, Minnie didn't see them for three days. When she did, she turned to Amy. "Those horses are Charlie's," she announced. "They're venom horses. And, they're due for an injection right now."

"Well, you'll have to take it up with Joe. I just know that he caught them out on the way to Shelby. They were staggering around on the highway from lack of water. Made it easy to pick them up."

"Amy, is it possible to keep the horses here until we get our fence put in out at Greasewood Junction?"

"Take it up with Joe, Minnie. It's fine with me."

"So, those are Charlie's horses?" Yellowhenry asked when next they met.

"Yes. They got out," Minnie said simply.

"What does Charlie need with five horses? There isn't enough feed out there on his property for one horse, much less five. What's going on, Minnie?"

"We're having a load of hay delivered in a few days. We've contracted to build a barn and a stable and to fence in forty acres."

"Charlie doesn't have forty acres, Minnie."

"We're gonna buy the extra ground," she said quickly.

"It's part of the Public Domain. They don't sell that."

"Well, our horses need that ground and if the Public Domain insists, they can come out and tell us to pull the fence. Are you gonna tell 'em?"

"Minnie, you and I did not have this conversation. Don't tell Charlie or James or Amy or anyone else. Is that clear?"

"What conversation? Who are you?"

"Take good care of James and Charlie so I don't ever have to come out there and see what isn't there. Kapish?"

"Radish," she grinned.

"You can keep your horses here. There's enough feed down in that lower pasture they like to hang out in for a few weeks. You might have to buy some hay eventually."

"I'll keep my eye on it, Joe," she smiled and stood on tiptoe to kiss his cheek.

For the next month the serum horses were processed at Yellowhenry's place.

Chapter 21

Amy and Yellowhenry had lulled into a platonic marriage. Neither objected to it. She was carrying his last child and she had suspended sexual relations, earlier than necessary. But it was what it was. They'd come to accept it and didn't give much thought to its return. They had six kids to raise which superseded all else. Affairs of the heart were notwithstanding. Control of the tamped down emotions was well in hand.

So, when he took a day trip out to the east and stopped off to say 'hello' to Carolyn Malone, he was astounded at how quickly his control fell off the rails. After a cup of coffee and a round of tossing her triplets into the air, she banished her kids to their playroom with her nanny. "Let's take a walk, Joe," she said.

"I should probably be getting on the road, Carolyn," he said.

"It's always 'probably' with you, Joe," she laughed. "That leaves a little space between 'probably' and 'must'. Let's take a walk to the barn." She was wearing low cut ankle-high western boots and a belted shin length blue cotton dress with a full skirt. She walked a little ahead of him and he noticed the swell of her firm rump. He felt his erection stir, but he kept walking anyway.

When they stepped into the gloom of the barn, she turned along the line of stalls. "The hay is in here," she said, opening the third stall and stepping inside. He followed her and watched as she stood with her back to him as she unbuttoned her dress. He quickly moved to remove his service belt and hat, both of which he set aside. She used her feet to pull off her boots, then she shrugged and dropped the dress to the floor. She reached behind her back and unhooked her bra which she tossed onto the dress. When she turned, she wore only her bikini panties. "Don't embarrass me by refusing me, Joe," she whispered as she stepped into his embrace.

"I won't, Carolyn," he said hoarsely. He held her for a moment, enjoying the taste of her mouth and lips. He reached for her breasts and rolled her nipples gently between his thumbs and forefingers.

She moaned and sank to her back on the dress pulling him with her. She jerked on his belt eagerly, helping him to pull his pants to his mid thighs. They simply pulled her panties aside and he took her in one deep thrust that threw her legs to grip the center of his back. He held the position without doing anything but pressing deeply into her for fear of ejaculating prematurely. When the urge subsided, he began a vigorous circular and thrusting motion. She dropped her heels to the hay and timed her own thrusts to his. He kneaded her breasts and inhaled her nipples. Their first release was simultaneous. They rested before resuming after he had also disrobed. She took him in the female superior position, and they followed that with rear entry.

The session lasted for about forty-five minutes. They wanted to make sure that both were totally spent. "I don't think I can get a fourth without quite a lot more time," he said as he rolled away to his back.

"So, how was I as a tumble in the hay," she giggled.

"Too damned good, Carolyn," he chuckled and turned to kiss her. "I'll help you get dressed."

"That's sweet, but what would you do?"

"Brush all the hay off your back."

Lost Deer was down at the small stream a quarter mile below the rimrock that was the site of his and Shot Once's cave. He was working on his piece of the doe hide. With the use of their hatchet he had scraped the remnant free of blood, fat, and tissue. Nevertheless, the hide was stiff as a board. Using the water and gravel of the stream he patiently kneaded the fragment until it was pliable. It was a painstaking chore to ring the water completely out of the hair and leather. When he was satisfied, he hiked back up the severe slope to the cave ledge to where it tapered into the slope of the shoulder of the mountain. From there, he walked along the ledge, working his way through the rockfall that littered the shelf of rock.

When he reached the entrance of the cave, he immediately saw that Henry was not in evidence. His rifle and piece of doe hide were still where he had set them off to the side, however. Lost Deer looked to the fire they kept burning at all times and was irritated that it was down to a few smoking embers. He spent a few minutes resetting the small blaze before checking the torches they had leaned against the wall off to the left of the fire. Where there were four, two remained.

Instant rage surged into Lost Deer's arms, legs, and stomach. An acid burn from a reflex action in his gut scorched his throat. "You son of a bitch," forced its way past his lips. The sudden realization of what he was about to do, however, made his legs feel heavy as he rose and strode across the cave to his rifle. Then, he turned and lit a torch in the fire before heading to the tube leading to the artists' chamber.

Henry had doused one of his torches to use as a charcoal brush. The other he held overhead to provide light as he approached the image of the Irish Elk. He had shortened his grip on the smoking torch he intended to use to brighten up some of the lines of the animal and its antlers. He had just begun to make a stroke when Lost Deer's bellow made him jerk backward and down to the seat of his ass.

The muzzle of Lost Deer's rifle, despite its being held into his hip, was centered on Henry's sternum. "Kenney," he tried to explain, "I was just going to touch up some of the lines. The real faint ones. Please, don't shoot me. Kenney, this ain't no capital offense!"

Lost Deer's face was a controlled mask of fury. "I told you I'd kill you if you even touched this monument from our ancestors. But you tried to do it anyway."

"No, no, Kenney," Shot Once whispered in a near panic. "That was for graffiti. I wasn't going to do that. This was just a little reparation. An improvement to what our grandfathers started. This wall isn't finished, Kenney. I don't think the ancients thought it was."

"The only addition you're adding to this place is your bones," Lost Deer snarled through his bared teeth. The boom of the rifle shot that struck him center mass, blew Shot Once to his back as Lost Deer was instantly deafened. One of Shot Once's torches struck the wall making an exclamation point just above floor. Lost Deer used his foot to smear it into a smudge. Then he stripped Shot Once and dragged his naked body to the back wall of the cavern where it bled out.

Lost Deer knelt in prayer, facing the artists' wall, before he picked up his rifle and the torches. "Rest in peace my grandfathers," he said even though he could not hear the utterance. He returned to the main cave where he set about policing the place. He tossed everything including the two pieces of deer hide over the edge into the brush. When he was finished, there was no vestige that he and Shot Once had been there. With his rifle in hand and Shot Once's cash in his pocket, Lost Deer made a backpack of Shot Once's clothes, into which he rolled some dried meat from the deer. With the second rifle slung over his shoulder, he set out for the Holland Lake trail.

Chapter 22

Yellowhenry continued his patrol to the eastern boundary of the Havre section. As he travelled, he reflected upon what he had just done. For some reason, he didn't feel like he deserved self-excoriation. He felt guilty, but he knew that if Carolyn wanted to go walking at some time in the future, he'd probably go with her again. He gazed at himself in the mirror and thought about what it all meant. Especially, he found the visage of Monti Collier's near nude figure coming into his mind's eye.

"God almighty," he mused. "I really need Amy back."

His two-way radio crackled at that moment, "Base to Captain Yellowhenry."

"Yellowhenry," he answered.

"We have a train derailment along with a traffic accident ten miles west of Saco. Immediate assistance requested."

"Ten-four. I'll respond. Yellowhenry clear," he returned, flipping on his lights and activating his siren. He drove a modest eighty mph occasionally hitting his warbler as he overcame slower moving traffic that hadn't moved to the shoulder of the road. When he reached the scene of the accident, another trooper from the Glasgow office was on the scene. The officer was attempting to separate a pair of men who had been fighting, trying to settle road rage differences. The officer, a man of middling size was pressed between the pair of pugilists, both of whom were very large men. That they were out of shape and had spent most of their adrenaline was apparent. They had managed to inflict some real damage upon each other, nonetheless.

With Yellowhenry's assistance, the officer was able to pry and shove the pair far enough apart to get the story from them. The first man on the scene had slowed down to look at a train derailment that had dumped some box cars into Nelson Reservoir. The second had come upon the scene and rear ended the first. The two had gone to fisticuffs. Their accident was reported by the railroad crew who were highly entertained by the bare knuckle contest on the highway.

What everyone forgot was a third vehicle. With the wreckers gone, the road cleared of debris, and the two scrappers seated in separate patrol cars, Yellowhenry called in to report and to advise that he planned to overnight in Glasgow. He asked that his wife be notified. "Will do, Captain. What's the story with the third vehicle?"

"What third vehicle?"

"The train crew reported a third vehicle."

"This is the first I've heard of it."

"Well, let me double check. Yeah. Three."

"All right. I'm on it. Clear. Goddamnit!"

Yellowhenry stalked to where Trooper Kevin Raymond was plundering his first aid kit as he doctored up the fighter sitting in the backseat of his cruiser with his legs swung out to the ground.

"What's up?" Raymond asked.

"There's a third vehicle involved here. Did you hear or see anything about it?"

"I haven't looked. Ever since I've been here, I've been trying to stop Bob, here, and the guy in your rig from fighting. Bob, did you see another rig go off the road?"

"Yaw, somethin' swerved when I knocked that prick over the centerline. Didn't see exactly where it went. The lucky bastard got in a lick that knocked me down for a second. Seems like the rig, small size car, hatchback, I think, went right, then left. Musta gone off up there somewhere." He pointed behind Yellowhenry's cruiser.

"All right, Kevin," Yellowhenry said. "I'll go take a look."

What he found astounded him. "Damnit to hell!" he exclaimed. The car, a late model Honda CRV, had swerved to miss the pugilists, overcorrected without hitting the shoulder, overcorrected again, and left the highway a hundred yards beyond Yellowhenry's patrol car. It was balanced on a ledge some forty feet above the waters of Nelson Reservoir. In the rear hatchback window which faced him squarely from where he stood on the shoulder of the road a hundred feet above, a pair of little girls crying quietly were looking directly at him.

He sized up the scene. A gradual rock and grass covered slope led down to a narrow shelf above a section of rock wall that formed a part of the containment basin of the reservoir. The driver of the Honda had dynamited the brakes as the car careened off the highway and shot down the slope to finally bang onto the shelf where it stopped with its front tires over the edge. What Yellowhenry couldn't tell was whether the car was teetering. He decided to run back and recruit the other three to assist in rescuing the girls.

"Hey, we got a serious problem," he shouted as he hustled back to the scene of the rearend wreck. "It's gonna take all four of us."

"Screw that," Bob growled. "I ain't doin' nothin' that has anything to do with that son of a bitch."

"Then, do it for yourself, Bob," Yellowhenry yelled. "There are a pair of little girls trapped in that car you caused to drive off the road. The driver is nowhere to be seen either. If the driver is dead, you are guilty of manslaughter. So, don't be stupid, Bob. If we lose those little girls because that car plunges into the water, you'll be charged with their deaths, too."

"Jesus, let's go," the man suddenly exploded to his feet.

The three ran back the way Yellowhenry had come. "I'll be right behind you, Kevin," Yellowhenry called. "I'll get Leon out of my car."

Leon Wright was an oil field worker who had been headed back to North Dakota when he'd rearended Bob Ross. Both were six feet, four inches tall and over 240 pounds. "I'm not helping that bastard do anything," he declared when Yellowhenry ordered him out of the car.

In an instant, he was shocked to find himself looking with crossed eyes at the muzzle of Yellowhenry's service revolver. "Get out you prick. I don't have time to explain why," he raged.

"I'm comin', I'm comin'," Leon squawked. "Point that thing somewhere else."

"I'll point it right up your ass on my second shot, you miserable son of a bitch. Get out of there," Yellowhenry suddenly vented.

"I said I'm comin'," Wright repeated.

As soon as he cleared the car door, Yellowhenry slammed it and blasted Wright with his shoulder, spilling him to his hands and knees. As the man scrambled back to his feet, Yellowhenry's booted foot caught him in the ass forcing him to stumble forward. He took off running to catch up to Ross and Trooper Raymond who were standing on the highway shoulder, staring down toward the reservoir.

With all four gathered and Yellowhenry's gun holstered, they set off down the slope toward the car. The first problem they faced was that the hatchback was teetering and the back door was locked and wouldn't open. Yellowhenry shouted at the girls to duck down. "You three, grab onto the roof rack," he ordered. "We can't let this car go over."

Then he picked up a foot sized rock and began a two-handed smashing in of the rear window. It took a while to get an edge in the sheet of safety glass that he could get his fingers under. He began pulling, causing the car to shift slightly. He yelled at Ross, "Bob, help me peel this damned window outta there."

With the two ripping at the glass, it finally popped out of the frame. Yellowhenry tossed it out of the way. "Come here girls," he called gently. At first they huddled timidly. "It's gonna be all right," he added. "Let's get you out of there. It isn't safe."

When they began creeping to him, the older of the two began sobbing. "Mama fell into the water and Daddy jumped in after her. They're down there."

Yellowhenry felt his skin crawl, but he forced himself to remain composed. "We'll get them back, honey," he said comfortingly, "but first, let's get you and your sister out of there."

With the sisters extricated, and safely seated below the shoulder of the highway, the men managed to open the hatchback's rear door. Yellowhenry jerked the spare tire out and set it aside. The officers detailed the prisoners to loading the rear compartment with rocks to stabilize the car. "Do you see 'em anywhere?" Raymond asked as he peered over the edge of the shelf.

"Not yet," Yellowhenry answered. "Are you much of a swimmer?"

"Barely tread water."

"Damnit, then, I'll go," Yellowhenry declared.

"Sorry, Joe," Raymond said. "What can I do to help?"

"Go back up top and care for those girls. Take my clothes, toss 'em into my car, and order a wrecker, an ambulance, and a rescue boat. Lock those two pricks in separate cars. Get help out here to take them to jail. Remains to be seen, but they could be guilty of manslaughter."

Yellowhenry stripped down to his tee shirt and boxer shorts. Then, he sat down and pulled his boots back on. He thanked his lucky stars that he had decided to air out his western boots and was wearing laceup over the ankle boots. He laced them tightly and double knotted the laces. With the spare tire gripped in a space in the rim, he wound up and threw the tire into the reservoir. It hit the water, splashed, and bobbed in place.

"Well," Yellowhenry said to Raymond, "here goes nothin'." He took three running steps and launched himself, feet pointed down toward the reservoir. As he sailed toward the water, it flashed through his mind, 'At least I won't smell like sex.'

Chapter 23

Kenney Lost Deer with two murders to his credit, but with a surprisingly clear conscience, was hiking in the dark past the Holland Lake Lodge which had closed down for the night. At the last moment, he turned back, pulled Shot Once's shirt over his head, and quietly walked to the front door. He carefully leaned both rifles against the double doors and faded back into the shadows.

The next morning the manager of the lodge, John Richland was shocked to find the rifles. He took them into his office and looked at the security tape. All he saw was a figure, whose face was completely covered, step out of the shadows and carefully lean the firearms against the door and then back away. Richland called the county sheriff's office and reported the unusual incident. The sheriff surmised that one of the two fugitives of the FBI's manhunt had come back out of the Bob Marshall Wilderness. He called Dolan Aimes in Missoula and reported what had happened. "We'll notify Kalispell and have them seal off the north. We'll send agents in through Seeley Lake," Aimes decided. "We might catch him still in the Swan Valley."

While the authorities were sealing the valley, Lost Deer who had hitched a ride to the south was out of the Swan River country. He had ditched Henry's clothing in a dumpster at the Holland Lake's Campground upper loop. He was on a bus with a one way ticket to West Stewartstown, New Hampshire. He would go through two changes of buses on his journey to a town he knew something about that was close enough to Canada so that he could scoot over the border if the heat got too close. His great aunt Cleo Bright Moon lived there. She was a seventy-six year old widow who lived alone. She also loved her great nephew. He lived with her until she died twelve years later. He inherited the house as Sidney Aldden, her late nephew on her maiden name's side of the family. He lived there and continued working as the custodian in an elementary school. His forty year career was exemplary, including many accolades for service. He never revealed the location of the cave containing Henry Shot Once's body. Neither did law enforcement find it. Lost Deer took his own life with a gunshot to the head ten days after he retired.

James Yellowhenry and Charlie Goodwoman were milking snakes at Charlie's clinic. Minnie was home at her residence on the reservation. Otherwise Charlie would never have included the twelve year old youngster in handling the snakes. "I'm only going to let you milk this one. It's the smallest one, James," Charlie was saying. "Now, these snakes, even little ones like this, are pure muscle. When you have hold of their head, they will wrap you as soon as they contact your arm. So, you always support their body with your left hand and arm if you are going to move them anywhere with a head grip. That keeps them from feeling like they are being dropped. They twist like hell when you only have them by the head. It's kind of like a cat being dropped. They always twist so they can land on their feet. Snakes are like that when they sense they're about to be dumped."

James, who had watched the procedure many times, asked, "Do you really need to tube a snake that small?"

"Yes. It's the safest way," Charlie answered. He was referring to the capture of snakes by inserting them headfirst into a clear plastic tube and slipping the tube over them until they could be grabbed by the body to keep them from backing out. Then, they could be safely moved to the milking table where they could be eased out onto the Teflon surfaced table so they could be gripped by the neck just behind the head and positioned to bite the latex covered venom collection vessels.

The technique was a three finger grip with the thumb and middle finger aside the neck and the index finger stabilizing the center of the snake's head. For righthanded milking, the body of the snake was supported by clamping it under the right arm and supporting the extended body with the left hand, providing a secure platform so the snake's concentration was on biting the elastic membrane instead of squirming around setting up to take a fall. The venom glands could be stroked with the index finger to maximize the collection.

With the three and a half foot specimen tubed, the pair trooped in their snake boots to the collection table. Charlie walked to the right of the table so James could work from the left bringing his right hand and arm into play. The table was one of the latest models, eight feet long, three feet wide, and capable of being raised and lowered with a foot pump. Venom collection was accommodated in ring holders for the vessels at the end of the table.

With James positioned on the left, Charlie began easing the tube off the snake. "Now, hold the snake firmly, but don't pinch his head off. There's a feeling for it. You're the boss, you're in control, you use pressure to stay there. As long as you support the body, you'll get an even smooth bite of the membrane. After the collection is completed, you'll step away from the table, and drop the snake into the collection chest. Now, James, that's when it gets a little tricky. You'll drop the snake all at once and clear your hand as quickly as you can. Snakes strike quick. When you turn loose of the head, throw it, spread your fingers as wide and as quickly as you can. Just like you've seen me do it dozens of times. Do you have that?"

"Got it," James said.

"All right," Goodwoman said, "here comes your snake."

Chapter 24

When he hit the surface after a forty foot drop, Yellowhenry was glad he was wearing boots. He knew how unforgiving the surface of water is, but he didn't expect it to feel almost concrete hard. Fortunately, he had pointed his toes as much as he could, so he sort of slipped into the water as opposed to ploughing in flat-footed. Still, he felt the jolt clear to the base of his skull. As soon as his momentum stalled he clawed for the surface. When he was back on top, he looked around for the spare tire. It was about thirty feet further out from shore, and he immediately swam to it and hoisted himself to his belly onto it.

He turned the tire toward shore and began looking around. At first, he saw nothing, and it panicked him into thinking that he was going to have to dive to try and retrieve bodies. He shielded his eyes and looked down into the somewhat murky waters of the reservoir. He saw nothing below him, so he began paddling, looking down as much as he could. He also scanned the shoreline which had flattened out and was crowded with brush and willows. After covering nearly a hundred yards, he turned toward shore and paddled back the way he had come. It was then that he saw a flash of white in the brush of the bank.

He began stroking strongly towards the site and was rewarded when he was able to ground the tire and stand up. A man wearing a long sleeved white shirt was kneeling in the sand above the brush line and keening silently as he rocked back and forth next to the figure of a woman laid out on her back. When he saw Yellowhenry, he rasped out with a voice nearly gone, "I fear she's dead."

Yellowhenry fell to his knees and pressed his fingers to the woman's neck seeking a pulse. He moved his fingers several times, testing both sides. He was about to give up when he found a very weak pulse. "Not yet," he bellowed and pressed his mouth to hers, blowing a firm breath that made her chest rise. Then he compressed her chest ten times and returned to her mouth. He kept at it as the man watched. A few minutes later, the woman farted and heaved upward. Yellowhenry rolled her to her side as she retched and belched out an unbelievable amount of water along with the contents of her stomach. When she finished, he eased her back and watched to see how she was breathing. He checked her pulse again and looked to the man.

"We've got her back," he said. "I believe she's going to make it."

The man looked at Yellowhenry and began blubbering, "Only you. Only you, Trooper Joe, could have saved Flora. She won't believe it. She has a poster of you in her bedroom. It serves as her inspiration. She'll believe you are a savior sent by God."

"Whoa!" Yellowhenry said, holding up his hands. "I'm no God sent anything. I'm just a lawman doing his duty. That's it. Enough with the rest of it."

He leaned down to check the woman's pulse. Just as he was pulling back, her arms shot around his neck and she pulled him into a passionate kiss. He twisted away as quickly as he could and peeled her arms from his neck. "I take it you're feeling better," he said.

"I was dead," she whispered. "Then I was being kissed and pumped, kissed and pumped. When I came to, I realized who was helping me. You're an angel, Joe, whether you know it or not."

"That's okay, Flora," he said. "I was just lucky to be the one to help. Your husband is your savior. He jumped into the water and got you out. Give him the credit."

Suddenly, Flora rose to her elbows, "My daughters," she cried.

"They're good, they're good," Yellowhenry said quickly. "We got them out of the car and they're safe with an officer of the highway patrol."

The man raised his hands skyward and cried, "Thank you Lord. Praise God."

"Praise Trooper Joe," Flora breathed. "He saved us all."

"Alrighty, then," Yellowhenry said brightly. "You know who I am. Who are you folks?"

"I'm Quentin Lightenger. Go by Quint. You know Flora. Boy, do you know Flora," he chuckled.

"Well, strange circumstances," Yellowhenry smiled. "Now, we need to check you two over for possible injuries. I saw that your airbags activated. So, no blunt force trauma, but you both hit the water from a long way up. We'll start with your own assessment. Flora, can you sit up and stand? Quint, you, too."

Quint rose easily and began checking his flexibility, bending his elbows and knees and leaning over from the waist as he twisted his back. He largely ignored the act Flora put on as she reached for Yellowhenry's hand to pull her up. She stood weaving on her feet, causing him to grip her forearm and reach around her back.

She leaned against him pressing her breast into his arm. Then she stumbled a bit as she took a step. He pulled her close to keep her from falling and she pressed her thighs against his leg as he stepped toward her to stop her fall. She wrapped her arms around his neck and pulled him toward her manipulating her stance to press her pubic bone firmly against his groin. Pretending to become faint, she ground into him as he bent first one way and then another to relieve the pressure and to get her off him. He finally managed to free himself and step away as she stood grinning at him. "I feel good now, Joe," she said.

Quint looked up from where he had finished his bends, flexes, and stretches. "So do I," he added. "Now, how do we get out of here."

"This rock wall ends about a quarter of a mile up the shoreline," Yellowhenry said. "We may have to swim part of it, but I have the spare tire from your car. We can all keep a hand on it, and paddle to where we can get out and walk."

It was then that Yellowhenry took stock of the two he was with. Quint was roughly thirty-five years old, five feet, eight inches tall, and stocky. He had brown hair and eyes, a round face, and he was dressed like a businessman. Flora was the same age and height, and Yellowhenry guessed her weight at 120 pounds. She was fair complexioned, had shoulder length blonde hair, and was built, as the old saying goes, like a brick shithouse. She was facially quite attractive. It didn't get by Yellowhenry that she was going to get as much feel off him as she could. That he was dressed in shoes, his boxers, and a tee shirt didn't help his evasive prospects any, either. He steeled himself for a groping.

Chapter 25

Charlie Goodwoman pulled the plastic tube quickly free of the rattler as James Yellowhenry seized it behind its head using his right hand to apply the three fingered grip in securing the snake's head. At the same time, he reached across his body with his left hand to grasp the snake's body and tuck it under his right arm. With the wriggling serpent firmly captured, he smoothly lifted its opened mouth to the edge of the plastic collection vessel where its dripping fangs bit firmly through the latex membrane stretched over the container. James stroked the bulging venom sacks on either side of the snakes head as it continued expressing its venom. "He's done, James," Goodwoman said after a few moments. "Dump him into the collection chest."

James pulled the snake's head free of the vessel, stepped away from the milking table, and neatly dropped the snake, throwing its head with a quick snap of his wrist. The snake, rattling madly, fell into the thigh deep chest. Charlie quickly slipped the form fitted lid onto the collection chest, and high-fived James. "Your first one, James. How do you feel?"

James, thrilled to the core, grinned broadly, "Scared," he said. "That's really exciting."

"Can you believe how strong your snake was?" Charlie asked.

"No. It's like grabbing a flexed muscle that moves and twists. I want to do another one," he said.

"Ah, let's not press our luck. We'll ease into it. There's a five footer coming up in a couple of days. You can watch me handle one of those next. We have one of the big ones to milk out today. The way you handle them is the same, except you add more support with your left hand. The strength of the big ones is something else. You have to be careful that you don't squeeze too hard on a snake's neck while you're putting extra pressure into controlling the body. The tendency is to add equal muscle to both your left and right as you overcome the struggles of the snake. Squeezing too hard behind their heads makes them go crazy."

"I thought mine was powerful," James said.

"Oh, he was strong, all right," Goodwoman said. "You were nice and smooth, though. Nice and smooth. Good job, James. The five footer, however, is a real thrill the first few times. It's just different. You'll see what I mean in a couple of days."

Minnie Graves was gravely concerned about the progress of Amy Yellowhenry's seventh pregnancy. Amy was at the end of her second trimester and she was experiencing false labor pains and spotting blood. "Have you talked to Joe about this?" Minnie demanded.

"No. It'll be all right," Amy answered. "He has enough on his plate to worry about without adding this."

"Look, if you don't talk to him, I'm going to. You need to go to a specialist in Billings, Amy. You can't ignore what's going on. You could be endangering your baby, to say nothing of yourself."

"I'm sure this is just a temporary condition, Minnie. This is our last baby, so all I have to do is take it easy for another sixty days. Then, if the baby wants to come early, that'll be just fine. They can give me a hysterectomy and I'll be done with it."

"Oh, my god," Minnie said. "The sublimity of the young and simple mind just blows me away. After your delivery, you'll have seven kids. Two who are nursing and you'll be flat on your back for five or six weeks while you recover."

"I won't be flat on my back," Amy protested. "I'll be restricted which will be eased off as I heal. It'll be fine. Don't raise a big fuss, Minnie."

"Like hell," Minnie declared. "I've helped you native girls for forty years through your pregnancies. Nine times out of ten, everything comes off without a hitch. But one time in fifty, something happens. Those girls who ignored the signs and thought they could just ride it out, like you're thinking, had one of three things happen. Do you want to know what those things are?"

"Not really."

"I knew you'd say that, Amy," Minnie said. "So pay attention. One, they lose the baby. Two, they die. Three, both die. I'm going to talk to your oblivious husband because he does not want to lose you."

"Don't be so sure, Minnie. We're in one of those lulls of affection right now," Amy said.

"Those happen in marriages. This has nothing to do with that. Love be damned for a while. I'm talking about your life. The mother to six kids. Don't be so damned selfish, Amy. Joe would make a mess of raising those kids without you. This is no time to be kind and deferential. It's life and death whether you see it or not."

"All right, Minnie," Amy sighed. "When he gets back from Glasgow, I'll talk to him."

"Good. I'll have your back. I'll give him hell, too."

Yellowhenry was leading but the trail petered out against a rock spur, forcing them back into the water. Flora was also beset by being absent one shoe she had lost in the reservoir. The trio trudged on, occasionally forced into the water where they used the spare tire to keep them afloat so they could make better progress against the drag of their clothing, especially that of the married couple. Quint plugged along, treading, and being dragged along by the efforts of the other two. Yellowhenry worked at arm's length doing his best to stay stretched out and away from the probing pinches and caresses of Flora. She pretty much had her way as she swung up onto the tire to be spilled off, grabbing Yellowhenry to get stabilized.

Her grabs were aggressive often inside his boxers. He staved her off at first, but finally resorted to simply slapping her hands away when she really overdid it.

When they finally reached a point to where they could climb up to the highway, Quint was exhausted. "Just stay here," Yellowhenry told both Lightengers. "I'll be back as soon as I can."

"I'm going with you," Flora announced. "My daughters will be going crazy."

"I'll tell them Flora, if they're still there. Chances are they've been taken to Glasgow."

"I don't care, I have to go see."

"Quint," Yellowhenry asked, "do you want Flora to stay with you?"

He looked up with dull eyes from where he sat on the shoulder of the road. "Go," he waved wearily. Then he said the oddest thing Yellowhenry could imagine. "Take Flora with you and keep on goin'. Take a minute or two and give her a quickie. It'll make her day."

That Flora didn't react was an even bigger surprise. "Come on, Joe. There's stuff going on you don't know about," she said.

Yellowhenry felt nearly naked as he began walking the half mile, plus, back to where he could see a police car pulled up along side the highway with the emergency flashers running. Traffic was stopped on the far side of the congregation of traffic as he and Flora began walking. "Look, Flora," Yellowhenry said. "You're private business is none of my affair."

"Quint and I are separated. We have been for a few months, now. This trip with the girls was a step to see about getting back together. He really wouldn't care if we did get it on."

"Well, there is a problem with that, Flora."

"Oh, what?"

"I'm married."

"Well, so am I. A little on the side is what America is all about, isn't it?"

"Can't argue with that," he said, feeling a sharp stab of recrimination twist his gut.

"I'll let you know where I'll be when this is all over," she said.

"Don't need it."

"Well, you're going to get it, anyway," she insisted.

Just then the cars from the other side came streaming through. They slowed and swerved aside as the drivers spotted the two bedraggled figures walking along the edge of the road. One of them pulled over and stopped. The driver was alone and he dropped the passenger side window. "Hey, Joe," he called.

Yellowhenry stopped, leaned down, and asked, "Mac, how're you doin'?"

"You're lookin' pretty rough. Can I give you and the lady a ride back there? It's most of a half a mile."

"No, that's all right, Mac. Getting turned around in this traffic wouldn't be the best. We'll be all right."

"All right," he said. "I'll read about it in the paper."

What Yellowhenry and Flora didn't notice was the cell phone documenters. A time or two she stumbled unintentionally when she stepped with her bare foot on a rock. He caught her as she hopped and leaned aginst him to check and make sure her foot wasn't cut. "You okay?" he asked.

"That hurt like hell," she said of the second one. By then they were within a hundred yards of the vehicle.

He bent over and said, "Hop onto my back, Flora. I'll carry you from here."

The pair surprised the trooper who had taken over for Kevin Raymond. He was parked near Yellowhenry's cruiser with its special paint job. "Jesus Christ almighty," he exclaimed, as he watched Yellowhenry walk up to his car and deposit Flora next to the driver's side door. "Trooper Joe. Everybody's been expecting a water rescue, and here you are on foot. What the hell happened?"

"A lot. Get on the horn and cancel the boat. Cancel the ambulance. A wrecker will be needed to pull that Honda up onto the road. There is a fella sitting beside the road about a half mile back. He'll need a ride. He can tell you where he needs to go and where the Honda needs to be towed. Where are those two girls we pulled out earlier?"

"They've been taken into Glasgow. A female officer has been assigned to their care," the trooper said.

"All right. As soon as I get dressed, I'll take this lady into Glasgow. She's the girls' mother. Do you have all that?"

"I'm on it. What's the fella's name I'm supposed to pick up?"

"Quint Lightenger. He and this lady are married, but they're going separate ways right now. Don't ask me why."

"Ten four, Captain."

Yellowhenry pulled his uniform from the back seat and dressed. Ten minutes later, with Flora in the passenger seat, they set out for Glasgow a little over fifty miles to the east. "Where am I going to stay tonight?" Flora asked. "Do you have friends or relatives in the Glasgow area," Yellowhenry asked.

"No. My purse is still in the car, too. Can't I just stay with you, Joe, please?"

"Nooo, you can't. I'm staying over and I'll get you a room in the same motel, but that's all."

"Are you hungry?" she asked.

"We'll have dinner after we've cleaned up. Sorry, you'll have to wear what you have on."

"That's okay. I'll wash out my bra and panties. I won't need them just to go to dinner. Then, I'll rinse out my dress when we get back. It'll all be dry tomorrow when we go to pick up my daughters."

"You don't want to see your daughters tonight?"

"I just want to tell them their father and I are okay and will see them tomorrow. I don't want to upset them about our latest breakup. They've been through enough. Will my purse be brought into the police station in Glasgow?"

"I'll see if we can get that handled." Yellowhenry called back to the trooper on scene and requested that he look for Flora's purse in the Honda and to bring it back to the office if he found it. Then he called the Glasgow patrol office and placed Flora's request about her daughters. "Is there anything else?" he asked.

"Just take me to a motel," she said wearily.

Chapter 26

James and Charlie Goodwoman were trying to corner a heavy five foot rattler that was refusing to crawl into the tube. "What do we do now?" James asked.

"Force him," Charlie said as he used his snake hook to pin the snake down a half foot behind its head. Then, he jammed the tube toward the head of the squirming reptile until it finally relented and entered the plastic orifice. Charlie slid his hand down the hook, let go of it and grabbed the snake's body six inches beyond where he had pinned it, and slid the body toward the tube as he pushed the tube toward his hand. With a foot of the snake inside the tube, Charlie kept adding more until he had half the snake captured. Then he carried the insanely rattling prisoner to the milking table.

James was fighting terror. His mouth had gotten so dry he was experiencing cotton mouth. He was leaking urine and his hands were shaking uncontrollably. If Charlie noticed, he didn't let it stop the procedure. "Now, James," he said. "Nothing changes except how strong a snake this size is. With his extra length, to keep him balanced, you have to reach further with your milking hand. He'll throw that extra length back at you. That will make you feel like he's pulling his head free. To stop that, use the rim of the collection bottle. Get him to bite the membrane. Be quick about it. That will straighten him out. One this big does require extra pressure in your milking hand and in how tightly you clamp your arm on him. Do not drop his body. Now, get ready. I'm going to de-tube him, but I'll pin his head for you with the hook."

Despite near numbing fear, James found his focus on the procedure all encompassing. With the snake's head facing the milking bottle, Charlie ordered James to control the snake's body as he eased the tube free and quickly slapped the head capture curve of the snake hook onto the snake's neck. "There you go, James. Pick him up," Charlie commanded.

Somehow, the kid did it. His Judo training transferred into function. He refused to be dominated. The snake twisted and air crawled with powerful thrusts of its body which James used to clamp its mouth onto the collection bottle. The big reptile bit and expressed its venom glands. Then it tried to recoil, but James forced it to bite again. He stroked its glands until no more venom shot from the rear of its fangs. Without instruction, he stepped to the collection chest and neatly deposited the pissed off, rattling and milked out serpent into its confines.

Charlie, who had been secretly on severe tenterhooks, bellowed, "That's how you handle the bad ones, James! Beautiful job, boy! Just goddamned beautiful!"

James beamed, but he held up his shaking hands. "I was scared shitless, Charlie," he laughed.

"I figured. But you didn't let it take over. That's the important thing, James. You were in charge, boy. Just a beautiful job. That's how you make money in this business, son. That's the money maker. You can't believe how proud of you I am."

"Thanks, Charlie," James enthused. "I really did all right, huh?"

"You sure as hell did. But, don't tell anybody just yet," Charlie said cautiously, as his thoughts flashed to how pissed off Minnie and Joe would be if they knew. "We'll want to get a few more under your belt first."

Chapter 27

Yellowhenry checked into the first motel he saw. The Glasgow Motor Inn was located on the west side of the town of 2,000 souls. As the county seat of Valley County, the town was able to maintain most of its population, unlike many other small towns in the country that were succumbing to the big box and online outlets that voraciously absorbed retail commerce and trade.

With adjacent rooms, Yellowhenry and Flora went about cleaning up to go to dinner. He saw with some trepidation the internal door that connected the two rooms. Shampoo was flooding his face when he felt her press against his back. "Damnit Flora," he yelled. "We can't be doing this."

He turned and she wrapped her arms around his neck, "Then, just stand still. I'll do it."

Despite himself, he was rock hard as she gripped him and inserted his erection. He was forced against the wall of the shower as she drove her hips as hard as she could, setting her feet to get maximum leverage. She climaxed first with a squeal that he was sure was heard in the office. He followed with his hands cupping her buttocks and grunts that coincided with lifts that pulled her feet off the shower stall floor. He held her clear of the floor as he leaned back and she entwined her legs around his. They held the pose as he expressed himself with both of them breathing like they'd just sprinted a foot race. "Now what?" he asked as he eased her back to her feet.

She pulled him into a lingering kiss. "Now nothing," she said when they parted. "Let's go eat."

With her freshly washed bra and panties hanging on the shower rod in her motel room, Flora looked at herself in the big mirror over the sink. Without her makeup, she saw something she hadn't seen in years. She was beautiful in a fresh faced kind of way. Her breasts were still firm with just a little help from her shoulders. Then she pressed her shoulders forward and her breasts dropped, noticeably so. The impression was definitely one of the opposites. It made her wish she had her makeup bag with her. At thirty-four, she didn't trust the freshness of nature.

Then, she slipped her dress over her head and let it settle. She had sponged as much dirt as she could off the garment. It was still wet in the bodice and clung to her. It was the next thing to transparent and made her smile in a slightly evil and provocative way. 'Hmmm,' she thought. 'Second course possibilities are still on tap.'

Flora walked into Yellowhenry's side of their suite to find him on the phone in an apparent argument with someone named Ames. It soon became clear that it was a personal thing and Ames was female.

He looked up and held up a finger to signal that he would just be a minute. He finally said, "I'm still in the middle of this thing. I should be home tomorrow night. I'll call if something comes up to delay me beyond that. I'll call you, Ames. I have to go. I'll call you. Love you, goodbye."

"Sorry," he said. "This layover was unexpected. My wife is a little upset. She'll get over it. She'll be okay."

"Well, I liked being 'this thing you're in the middle of,'" Flora grinned. "And I promise you, tomorrow I will be 'that thing.'"

"Jesus, Flora," he moaned. "I'm in over my head already. Let's not make it worse."

"Oh, like hell. You are in waist deep at the deep end of our pool. It won't get any deeper, so unless you do something to turn me off, count on doing some more paddling. I promise you'll never forget it or regret it. Now, take me to dinner and ply me with wine."

Dinner at Durum's was a relaxed pleasure, albeit a barefooted one for her. Flora's dress dried out and became quite modest, much to Yellowhenry's relief. They confided in each other about the problems that were besetting them, maritally. In the restaurant they sat on opposite sides of their table and were models of decorum. Yellowhenry was recognized three or four times. He was cordial and friendly, but he refused to sign an autograph on one occasion. His manner was so apologetic that the lady smiled and said she was sorry for asking.

Back at the motel, they entered in separate doors. Flora took time to wash her dress and hang it out to dry. Then she put on her panties and bra and walked into Yellowhenry's side. There, she wore the garments for only a half hour, or so.

The next morning Flora met her daughters at the police station and was presented with her purse and makeup bag. After filing paperwork and checking in with his office, Yellowhenry drove Flora to Wolf Point, fifty miles to the east. He walked Flora and her daughters to their small apartment. The girls evaporated into their shared bedroom, leaving the adults to themselves. Flora stepped into Yellowhenry's embrace. He turned his head so that her kiss brushed his cheek.

"First sign of disaffection," she sighed. "I knew it was too good to last."

"Flora," he said, "you have turned out to be a breath of fresh air, despite our rather strange beginnings."

"I wasn't taking no for an answer, Joe," she grinned looking into his eyes. "I am so glad I didn't."

"Are you going to be all right?" he asked.

"Oh, yeah," she said mischievously. "Delightfully sore for a few days."

"Yeah, well, me, too," he chuckled. "God, what a rodeo."

She giggled. "The bull riding was sensational."

"Ah, well," he said, "before things get out of hand again, what I meant was how are you doing for money. I know you're looking for work. You are without wheels. Does your husband pay you support?"

"Very sporadically. I have to leave here. I'm going to catch the bus and head west. My first stop is going to be Havre."

"Havre? Oh, boy. Why Havre?"

"I have a job interview with a veterinary clinic there. Scheduled for next week."

"Is that where Quint was taking you?"

"That was the general idea. Sort of got derailed. He is a pharmacist from Glendive. It was a big deal for him to take us to Havre."

"How did you get up here?"

"Took a job as a school nurse. Doesn't pay the bills despite job satisfaction."

"I have an idea, Flora. If you are moving by bus, whatever you're loading on the bus will fit in the trunk of my car. I'll drive you to Havre myself if you can leave today."

"Are you serious?"

"Absolutely. I'm deadheading back. It will save you bus fare for the three of you. Why not?"

"Yeah, okay, Joe. The girls and I can be packed in half an hour."

"Great," he said, kissing her impulsively. "I'll load while you pack."

With the car packed, they were on the road an hour later. "You know your police cruiser is beautiful, Joe. But that console takes all the romance out of it," Flora teased from her seat against the passenger door.

"Let's call it a safe distance," he said.

"First time in two days," she said. "I know what it means, too. I'll behave, Joe. That's a promise."

"I'm going to hold you to it."

Chapter 28

Yellowhenry finally made it home an hour after shift. He found himself bone weary and strangely normal. He hugged Amy over her belly in an arm extended A-frame and kissed her passionlessly. "How is our lucky seven coming along?" he asked.

"Just fine despite what Minnie is going to tell you."

"What?" he said. "What does that mean?"

"It's just woman things, Joe."

"I'll be back in a bit."

"Where are you going," she asked.

"To talk to Minnie. I need to know what's going on that you aren't going to tell me."

Her protest fell wasted on his retreating back.

"Well, it's about time you woke up," Minnie said indignantly. "Amy's in trouble with this one. False labor and bad spotting. She's in constant pain, and she thinks she can tough it out for another two months and have a cesarean section. She refuses to ask you to take her to a specialist in Billings and find out what the hell is going on. No midwife is going to handle this, Joe. I'll take care of your kids except for Waylon. You three head for Billings as soon as you can get an appointment. Take her to emergency services if they try to run you down the road a month. You could lose them both, Joe. There's something seriously wrong with this pregnancy. I've been midwifing for going on forty years. I know what I'm talking about."

"Thank you Minnie. I'm taking her tomorrow."

"Something else you should know."

"About Amy?"

"No. About James. He's milking snakes. And before you go postal about it, he's a natural. He's better at it than Charlie is. He needs your support not your condemnation. He will own and operate that place by the time he gets out of high school. As a licensed herpetologist with his own clinic, he'll make a quarter of a million a year, and add that much to his business every year, too. So, don't you go getting in his way."

"All right, I won't. Is there antivenin at the clinic with syringes that aren't rusted shut?"

"Yes, Joe. I've seen to that."

After overnighting in Billings, the OB/GYN Yellowhenry threatened with his life the next morning was Dr. Desmond Blasingame. When he realized that Yellowhenry was a famous captain with the Montana Highway Patrol, he became Dr. Stepan Fetchit.

With his one year old and his eleven year old daughter, Susie, to help out, Yellowhenry spent most of that day prowling the waiting room at Billings Clinic Hospital. The doctor ordered a complete battery of tests, including blood work, pelvic examination, and ultrasound followed by X-Rays. An MRI was scheduled for the following day. When Yellowhenry tried to get early results, he was told that everything was still in process.

Amy was just as confounded as her husband. She nursed Waylon every three hours and every session she tried to pry answers from Yellowhenry, whom she was sure knew something she didn't. It was Susie who finally stopped the inquisition when Amy became angry almost to the point of shouting. "Mom, just shut up!" she said. "I've been with Dad all day and I've heard what they've told him. Nothing. So, leave him alone. He'll tell you as soon as he knows something."

Amy looked at her daughter and began laughing. "Okay, I'm zipping my trap. Joe, I'm sorry. I'm just so worried about all this. I wish you'd just take me home. I'll lay in bed for the rest of the term."

"Honey," he said. "One more day and we'll do what's best for us. If it's bed rest, that's what we'll do, but let's hear what the doctor has to say tomorrow."

The family was turned loose late that afternoon and Yellowhenry dropped Amy, Waylon, and Susie off at their motel while he went out for takeout food. After they'd eaten, they watched a movie on TV. It was only 7:30 when Amy pulled the pin on the day. She gave Waylon a final feeding before she went to bed. Within minutes she was sleeping soundly.

"Dad," Susie asked with tears welling in her eyes and spilling down her face, "is Mom gonna be all right."

"Yes, sweetheart. We just have to figure out how to get her baby through this."

"If it comes down to a choice, Dad, you've got to save Mom."

"Of course," he said, choking up, "of course Mom comes first."

Chapter 29

Flora asked for her interview with the Hill County Veterinary Clinic to be conducted the next day. The clinic agreed, and she was interviewed by Dr. Nancy Arbordooven. The position that had unexpectedly come open was for a receptionist and intake server. Flora crossed all the T's and dotted all the I's. After an immediate second interview by the owner and lead veterinarian, Dr. Ronald Boston, she was hired on the spot. Her job was an hourly position at twenty-eight dollars an hour. A fortune in her eyes. She was given scrubs to take home and wear over her clothing when she reported for work. She was to start the following day.

Using her cell phone, she called for a cab to take her back to her hotel room. She asked the cabbie to wait for a minute while she rushed inside to get her daughters. "I got the job," she squealed. "Come on, we're going to go buy a car."

Two hours later, the three females were driving around town in a bright yellow used Toyota Camry. They were looking at houses and apartments for rent. Flora was especially interested in settling where her daughters could walk to school or to a school bus stop. She found what she was looking for in a furnished duplex on the north side of town. It was only a mile from her work. She was going to have to pay a hundred dollars a month more than her apartment in Wolf Point, but it was a three bedroom, two bath with a furnished laundry room. With her job paying her sixty thousand dollars a year, she was a nearly independent woman in the chinks.

The Lightengers moved in immediately. Flora and her daughters celebrated that night with pizza and a TV movie. As she lay in bed trying to wind down from the whirlwind of the last three days, Flora couldn't stop thinking about Joe Yellowhenry. She had no intention of trying to keep up their relationship, even on the sly. But he had turned her head completely away from Quint. She would let the divorce go through. Her poster of Yellowhenry, one of a kind she'd had made a couple of years ago, looked down on her from the ceiling above her bed. It stirred her as it always had, but now the images that came into her mind's eye were not imaginary. They were much more than that. As she drifted into slumber, Flora Lightenger was a woman in waiting.

Results of Amy's MRI were not positive. While the final analysis was a week away, Dr. Blasingame revealed in a private conference with Yellowhenry that there was an underlying problem with Amy's health aside from her pregnancy. "Her white blood cell count is sharply elevated," he said. "That is troubling."

"Meaning what?" Yellowhenry asked.

"What I fear is that your wife has cancer."

Yellowhenry was stunned. "Will she survive? What kind is it? How will it affect the baby? Should she be nursing our one year old? What if we abort the baby right now?" he asked without giving time for Blasingame to answer.

"Let's take it a step at a time," he answered. "Yes, she will survive. I suspect it's cervical cancer. It won't affect her baby. Her milk is probably safe, but I would advise switching your one year old to formula, just to be on the safe side. Abortion is unnecessary, but I would advise a full hysterectomy at the time of delivery. I also advise a cesarean section. Say, in five weeks. Her baby should be placed on formula at birth. I'll recommend one that is prescription based so you can obtain it with insurance benefits. Stock up here where it's available. It may not be up your way."

"Why can't we just buy the stuff on the grocery shelves?"

"Not all over the counter formulas have good nutritional value, especially for newborns," he answered wryly.

"What about the formula for our one year old?"

"I'll recommend two. Both OTC. They have different flavors and neither is commonly available throughout the state of Montana. I'd suggest you get a three month supply here in Billings. Split the choice between the two so your one year old can decide which he likes better. You can mix the one he doesn't like with the formula for your baby. That way, it won't go to waste. Then, you can grab what he likes the next time you're here in Billings. I want to see your wife weekly, if possible, until we take the baby."

"If you can schedule her early Monday mornings, it would help. We can drive down on Sundays and back on Mondays. I'd only be out of my office one day a week that way," Yellowhenry offered.

"I'll see to it. Now, let's go see Amy."

Amy's reaction was subdued, apparently stoic. "Please write all this down Dr. Blasingame," she said when he'd finished his summation.

"I will," he said. "I'll also include a list of conditions which will trigger your immediate need to return for surgery. Your baby is viable now, so we can operate without endangering it at any time. It's just best to wait as long as we can. Now, if father and daughter can give us a private moment?"

"Come on Susie," Yellowhenry said. "We'll wait in the lobby."

"Haven't you said enough?" Amy demanded of the doctor.

"I know, but this is something you can share with your husband out of earshot of your daughter. Your further sexual encounters are to be protected by either dental dams or condoms. I do believe you have cervical cancer which is, in your case, isolated and very treatable. You can still enjoy sex, but let's make it as safe as possible," Blasingame said.

"My husband and I have suspended sex for quite a while now. I'm not missing it at all, and if nothing changes, I'll find other ways to satisfy him, or I'll look the other way if he strays."

"That is not something I offer advice about. If you'd like to avail yourself to family counseling, I can recommend such services."

"Forget it doctor," she said. "Up on the reservation, we have our own way."

"Of course," he said.

Chapter 30

An uneasy routine settled in at the Yellowhenry household. Minnie Graves spent more and more time there, helping Amy with her kids. Dr. Blasingame advised Amy to use a breast pump in conjunction with switching Waylon to formula. The change wasn't easy and Susie was proven instrumental in guiding the little boy into his new food choice. Solid baby food was also incorporated into his diet. Overall, the work wasn't difficult but it was unending.

Yellowhenry wasn't really looking for a male confidant, but he found one in Art McClintock. How the conversation was broached, Yellowhenry wasn't sure. The pair was having a closed door evaluation and review meeting about the officers assigned to the Havre office. They had kicked back with cups of coffee and were just visiting. "Why haven't you ever married, Art?"

"Too ugly."

"Ah, come on. You had to have had opportunities."

"I suppose so when I was younger. Just didn't happen. I was always concerned about my woman looking at other men. No confidence in myself."

"Makes you wonder why it happens so often, doesn't it?" Yellowhenry asked.

"Oh, not really. Sixty-five percent of all marriages end in divorce. A lot of them are through infidelity on the part of one partner or the other. Maybe both. I just never really understood that whole thing."

"Why would you say that?"

"Well, man is really by instinct like most other animals. The real purpose for all species is to keep themselves going. Man thinks he's different because he chooses to follow rule makers. Law and order guys like us cops to control behavior, and religious rule makers to make us feel like guilt ridden sinners when we break their rules."

"Why, do you suppose, way back when, those rules were adopted?"

"They were frightened by the law of the jungle which meant only the strongest males were allowed access to the females. The herd of the denied, could only prevail through intellect. Somehow, they pulled it off. In most Christian cultures, they decreed one man and one woman united totally and forever. That assured even the least fittest a breeding partner. They invented hell and damnation and a soul doomed to the fires of the devil for all eternity if that man or woman even thought of having sex with someone else. Avoid that thinking and you were good to go. But, if you didn't, you could go to church and confess your sin to your pastor or priest and reclaim your spot on the narrow path that leads to another imaginary place called Heaven. I mean, they had to have a practical way to gain redemption, or the system would simply be unmanageable. It would fall apart from within. Too many people would have said to hell with it and it would have been back to the law of the jungle."

"Yeah, when you think of it, Man seems to be the exception to the rule," Yellowhenry said.

"Look at most species, especially mammals. The biggest and strongest do the breeding most of the time. Even the inferior females, like in wolf packs, don't often breed. In other words, the strongest breed to give the species involved the best chance to survive and sustain. Man doesn't do that," Art continued. "By spreading the joy to all members he has managed to breed himself into the unique position of being one of the most endangered major species on the planet. Some scientists say the one species most in danger of extinction due to overpopulation."

"I never gave it that much thought, I guess," Yellowhenry said. "Against that background, our breeding habits are an exception."

"Well, they are. Most mammals have breeding seasons. We are plagued by the urge to breed all the time. Raises hell when it runs up against the rules. I have to say, I'm amused by the rule makers who break their own rules. All those religious types out there porking the kids while giving men and women holy hell for even thinking about infidelity. No. I just said to hell with it. I'm tortured enough without adding that to it."

It didn't give Yellowhenry a pass for his infidelity, but it eased his general conscience somewhat. He knew that Amy had had thoughts of infidelity. He clung to that to avoid driving himself to drink or to go crazy. At the same time, he rededicated himself to her and their family.

Their trips to Billings became a pleasant interlude for them. They left Waylon at home since he was no longer breast feeding. Susie stopped going out of boredom, so the two of them simply fell in love all over again. Their Sunday nights were devoted to small talk, cuddling, and private methods of giving each other gratification.

Chapter 31

Under Charlie's watchful eye, whose eye was under Minnie's watchful eye, James gradually achieved more skill, knowledge, and confidence in all aspects of running the clinic. The only time he really had a chance to show off occurred when he injected the venom horses or drew blood from them. Of course his younger siblings and friends in the neighborhood flocked to see the procedures. The most exciting part of it was actually rounding up the horses and getting them to stand in place so the procedures could be completed. None of the horses had actually been completely gentled.

With Yellowhenry's help, Charlie had built a chute with a short wing, a pivot gate, and a set of pole pockets against the side of the corral. The horses were eased one at a time into the chute which was shut off by the pivot gate. Four poles were then passed behind the horse into the pockets. Three of the horses settled down and submitted to the indignities inflicted upon them, but two hated the needles and reared and bucked in the chute.

The assembly had gathered to watch a blood draw, which was always done in the evening so that Yellowhenry could help. After the three manageable horses had been run through, the first of the two wild ones was trapped in the chute. It was a young palomino stallion that squealed, grunted, and bucked straight up and down until it reared, planting its head and forelegs over the top rail of the chute. Yellowhenry was dressed in cowboy togs, including an old, felt western hat. He began flogging the horse's head and eyes until it dropped back down in the chute. "Let's leave him alone for a while," he said.

"Damn you, Charlie!" Minnie shouted. "I told you to get rid of that one and that bay mare."

"I just want to draw blood one more time so we don't waste the serum, Minnie. Then, I'll see about getting replacements. Damnit. They'll be out of cycle with the other three, though."

"Charlie," Yellowhenry said. "do you have knockout meds with you?"

"Yeah, why?"

"Let's nut that hammer headed son of a bitch."

"Can we do that with him down in the chute?"

"Won't even try it. We'll dose him and turn him out. When he goes down, we'll secure him with rope and do it then."

"Okay," he said. "Do you think that will help."

"Yes, I do. Geldings are just easier to work with. We'll also tie that mare up here in the corral and I'll start working with her, sacking her out. By the time you're ready to draw blood again, we'll lead her in with a halter."

"He just saved your ass, Charlie," Minnie growled.

By the time the palomino finally collapsed, the bay mare had been fought into the chute into submission, haltered, and tied to the side of the corral.

Then, Yellowhenry tied up a hind leg on the supine stallion and castrated him. From his years as a farrier and overall amateur horse doctor on the reservation, he still carried KRS, a medication for warding off flies and treating cuts, abrasions, and castration wounds to both cattle and horses. He doped up the twin gashes to the stallion's empty scrotum, James drew its blood, and they waited for the horse to come out of the sedation. Charlie admitted he had only guessed at the strength of the knockout dose. He also admitted he didn't have any medication to reverse the sedative. When the palomino hadn't shown any signs of recovery within a half hour, everyone left but Yellowhenry.

He decided to keep the entire herd of venom horses in the corral overnight. He threw down some hay from the loft and spread it out in the corral. For the bay mare, he pulled his galvanized tub from his back porch and dumped water into it. She pulled hard against the halter and showed the whites of her eyes, but he ignored her. He tossed a big flake of hay to where she could get at it, then he took a seat in the breezeway of the stable and waited for the palomino to revive. He finally went to bed at midnight with the horse still down. It was breathing, so the obvious conclusion was that Charlie had given the horse a dose that would have knocked out an elephant.

When Yellowhenry checked on the horses the next morning, the palomino was up but on very wobbly legs. "Damn you, Charlie," Yellowhenry growled. "This is an object lesson that isn't going to waste." He walked back to the house and rousted James. "Come with me, Son," he said. "There's something in the corral you need to see."

"Is the palomino staggering because you cut his nuts off, Dad?" he asked.

"No, Son. He's lucky to be alive because Charlie gave him a dose that would have dropped an elephant. He admitted he just guessed at the dose. I know you're learning the ropes out at the clinic, but you need to learn the science, too. The proper ratios of medication to the size of the animals you're working with. I don't ever want to see an animal mistreated like that palomino because you didn't learn from Charlie's mistake. Snakes excepted. I would never say anything if you over doped a snake."

"I get it, Dad. I don't ever plan to have pet snakes, either. Charlie keeps trying to tame them, though."

"Well, there's your first lesson in doping. Figure out how much antivenin you're gonna have to inject him with when he gets bit. Figure out the dose you'll need when you get bit. That brings up another subject. We're going to teach you how to drive."

"I'm not old enough, Dad."

"I didn't say legally. If Charlie gets bit and can't drive, it'll be up to you. In a life and death situation, you won't have a choice. I'll get Charlie started on that right away. To start, you'll just drive the road into and out of his place. Then, I'll see about a special exemption so you can drive to the hospital. Now let's halter that palomino. I'm keeping him in the stable for a couple of days."

Chapter 32

For the next month, the pair of half wild horses did, indeed, suffer the gentling process exacted upon them by Yellowhenry. After two weeks, James got in on the act. The sacking out process was just what the term described. Using burlap bags, Yellowhenry conditioned the animals to human touching. At firt he blindfolded the pair of horses, followed by rubbing them down with the sacks. He had to avoid front leg strikes as well as rear leg kicks that nearly whistled in their wickedness. The process included flicking the knotted end of a rope at their heels. At first, the horses double kicked and thrashed, pulling hard on their headgear.

Yellowhenry spoke to the horses in a calm assuring voice. After the initial gentling, he began rewarding with carrot chunks which allowed him to begin hands-on familiarization. James came in at that point and increased the process. There was a point at which the horses seemed to cross a watershed. James and the palomino struck up a mutual trust such that the horse would walk around the corral following the youngster, nudging his shoulder in hopes of a carrot treat.

"Dad," James asked a month into the process, "do you think I'd ever be able to ride Pal?"

"I don't see why not. You're, in effect, his owner. You should check and make sure that wouldn't affect his value as a venom horse, though."

"Okay," the boy said excitedly. "I'll research the physiology and find out."

The time had finally arrived for Amy's C-section. Minnie was given charge of the kids. Susie, Amy, and Yellowhenry with a full box of baby diapers, a supply of prescription grade formula, and a box of disposable baby bottles, plus clothing for a week for all of them, set off for Billings.

The procedure was scheduled for early Monday morning. The family checked into their motel on Sunday afternoon. Yellowhenry and Susie did their best to lift Amy's spirits, but a dark mood that had percolated into her psyche over the previous two weeks setttled in even more profoundly.

While she didn't cry openly, she wept almost constantly. "Ames," Yellowhenry said holding her closely. "You're overdoing this. Why are you so upset?"

"It's a sense of doom. I can't explain it, but if it happens, promise me you'll marry Carolyn when the time is right."

"Stop it, Amy!" Yellowhenry blurted in shock. "Just stop it. You aren't going anywhere, and I will not talk to you about future wives. I will not do it, so just drop the subject."

"Okay, but I've said it."

The C-section came off without complications. The hysterectomy was performed smoothly and to Dr. Blasingame's complete satisfaction. A five pound nine ounce healthy baby girl was cleaned up and whisked off to the maternity viewing ward. Amy was returned to her room where she was monitored for recovery.

Susie and Yellowhenry stood together and gazed at the newest member of their family. Four other infants lay sleeping in adjacent infant beds. Two were boys, one white and one black. "How long will it take before they aren't so ugly, Dad?" she asked.

He laughed, "I think your little sister, Amy Clara, is beautiful right now. She'll only get more so as she grows. But it takes a couple of months. You remember from your brothers and sisters."

"I didn't pay attention to them, Dad. Amy is the first one I'll actually have much to do with. Why are you naming her Amy? That's Mom's name."

"To honor your mother, sweetheart," Yellowhenry said. "This is her last baby. Besides, your mother is Mom."

"Yeah, I guess so. But, those two boys in there look squished."

"So would Amy if she'd been born naturally and weighed nine and a half pounds," he chuckled.

After ten minutes of watching their baby, the pair went back to the waiting room. An hour later Dr. Blasingame came into the room and, smiling happily, reported that all was well. "Your wife is awake and giving your daughter her first feeding. You can go in, but wear a mask, just for the baby's sake. Without natural colostrum and being premature, she will be susceptible to illnesses until her formula, which has colostrum added, kicks in. Your wife deferred to you for the baby's name."

Yellowhenry wrote the name out for the birth certificate and Blasingame left. "Well, Susie, let's go see if Mom will let you share in feeding Amy, shall we?"

Amy looked at her husband and daughter with tears in her eyes and a wan smile on her lips. "There you are," she said. "Joe, she is so beautiful. I know you wanted a boy. You aren't too disappointed, are you?"

"Of course not," he said. "She looks so much like her mother; she already has my heart."

Susie crawled onto the bed, being careful not to snug the blankets too tightly around her mother. "Would you like to help feed your sister, honey?" Amy asked.

"Yes," she answered eagerly, "Dad said you would let me."

"Your father knows me too well," Amy laughed, shifting the baby and bottle to her daughter. "What did you name her, Joe?"

"Middle name, Clara."

"Kind of old fashioned, honey," she smiled.

"First name. Susie, you tell her."

"Amy. Mom, I love it," Susie said.

"Whatever made you do that, Joe?" Amy asked, completely surprised.

"You," he said huskily. "To honor everything you are to your children. I couldn't think of anything else close to this."

"Kiss me, Joe," she said, tears cascading suddenly.

Chapter 33

Yellowhenry and James were working on Pal's first ride. The horse was skittish and fighting the snaffle bit. James rode Hi Boy and watched his father train Pal how to rein and stop on command. The palomino had a tendency to try and bolt. At first the conflict between Yellowhenry and the horse caused the animal to rear and crow hop. Each time Yellowhenry pulled Pal's head hard to the left, causing him to circle until he was under the control of the bit.

The ride they had staked out was from their house and up the bottom of the drainage where Minnine and Charlie hunted snakes. They planned on two hours out, and hopefully, less coming back. The outward part was more arduous than what Yellowhenry had hoped for. The wild streak in the recently gelded horse was still stronger than what he'd imagined it would be, but it was also the sign of a good horse in the making. As a result, the outward bound was extended for another hour.

When they finally stopped, as much from running out of terrain as anything else, Yellowhenry announced, "Okay, James. You ride him back."

"I'm afraid he'll buck me off, Dad."

"Son, you're handling five foot rattlers on a regular basis. One horse shouldn't be a match for you. Just clamp your legs and jerk his head back to the left. Don't let him duck his head. That could cause him to really buck. It that does happen, don't be afraid to grab the horn."

James was careful, turning his horse back several times and smoothing him back out. Yellowhenry had placed a rope around Pal's neck to stop a runaway. What he hadn't planned was a surprise of the type that was not unusual for horse backers in the Havre region. A rattlesnake had set off a warning which Pal used as an excuse to unexpectedly bolt. Yellowhenry checked him down, but Pal dropped his head and began to buck wildly.

At first James was thrown painfully between the pommel and high pitched cantle of his saddle, but somehow he caught the rhythm of the horse's front quarter's leaps and the kickouts of his rear legs. Pal's bucking was close to the quality of good rodeo horses.

Yellowhenry rode Hi Boy alongside like a pickup rider without crowding the bucking horse. At one point, he caught Jame's grin. At no point after he found his seat in the thirty seconds of the explosion was James in danger of being bucked off.

Pal gave up bucking by trying to bolt, but Yellowhenry and Hi Boy brought him around with an elated James who also pulled his horse's head up with his reins. "James?" Yellowhenry yelled, "Are you all right?"

"That was fun," he called back. "I'll be ready any old time he wants to do it again."

"Oh, my god, Son," Yellowhenry began laughing in relief, "I saw you grinning in the middle of that. Are you crazy?"

"Maybe, but that was a rush like milking my first rattler, Dad. That was wild, but this was just as good in a different sort of way."

"Son, don't tell your mother, but you might want to think about trying out for the high school rodeo team."

"Yeah, Dad," James exulted. "I'd really like to."

The ride back was uneventful, and Pal levelled out except for excessive head throwing. "Don't worry about that, James," Yellowhenry said. "We'll fit him with a martingale."

"When can we go riding again, Dad?" James asked.

"I can usually go on weekends, Son," Yellowhenry answered, "but Pal needs to be ridden as often as possible until snow flies. A couple of times a week, plus our ride on weekends. Can you fit that in with your school and clinic work?"

"Can I make him buck, Dad?"

Yellowhenry reached and ruffled his son's hair. "What do you want? A good horse, or a bucking horse good for nothing."

"A good horse."

"That's what I thought. Don't plant the bucking idea in his head. Let's fit him with a martingale, so you can take him out on your own."

Chapter 34

Amy's recovery was slow but steady. Susie and Minnie were great help when they were available and they tried their best to give her cover at all times. To fill in gaps, Carolyn Malone helped. Her nanny would take care of her triplets, allowing Carolyn the latitude to help Amy when Susie was in school and Minnie was at the Greasewood Serpentarium, as the place had finally been named.

It was during one of the final times that Carolyn was there because Amy was nearly fully recovered that Amy asked Carolyn to sit down for a cup of coffee before she left for her ranch. "What's wrong, Amy?" Carolyn asked.

"It's about my cancer," she replied. "It's treatable, but my shelf life is down to five, maybe seven years. I've reconciled myself to it. But, Carolyn, I will not waste down to where I look like a survivor of Dachau."

"Amy, that makes me think you are planning your suicide," Carolyn exclaimed.

"It's not a plan at the moment. That will come later. I am, however, taking you into my confidence. I don't know if you and Joe got it on when you crawled into his bed, or you did it later. I just know. And I don't care, Carolyn."

"Amy, we did not have sex when I slept behind him," Carolyn said, guilt splashing her face as she turned deep red.

"Let me finish, Carolyn," Amy insisted. "I've already told Joe that I want him to marry you after I'm gone."

"Oh, for heaven's sake, Amy," Carolyn cried. "Why did you do that?"

"For my kids, Carolyn. I know I've shocked both of you. I'm not giving up my marriage, but I know Joe was turned off for awhile. Right now we are madly in love again. I'm so grateful for it. But I have to be realistic. My kids are going to need a good stepmother. You, Carolyn. You. In time, Joe will put my passing behind him because of our kids. He won't have a choice. I want you to join Joe in doing what's right if you find it in your heart to love him. I know you have given yourself to him. That's a good start. I hope it's not wasted currency on down the line."

"Amy, I don't know how…" Carolyn began in an apologetic tone.

"Don't Carolyn," Amy said fiercely. "I almost did Trooper Abernathy. Someone walked in on us or we would have been down on the floor like a couple of cats. I forgive you and I forgive my husband. I know how it is. Please, don't make this harder on me than it has to be. This isn't going to happen right now. This is just the best time to take a hard look at the cards on the table. I'll never speak of this again. I hope you will not cast me out."

"Never, Amy. Never," Carolyn said firmly, reaching out to grip Amy's hand.

The rides on Pal were going nicely, although James did get him to buck on two occasions. He rode his palomino both times to a standstill. After that, the horse refused to do so much as crow hop. "You're no fun," James told the horse, but he made sure the ride was completed. In three weeks, the snaffle bit was replaced with a curb bit. "What bit comes next, Dad?" James asked.

"The next one is a spade. I don't believe in those because they are cruel to the horse. They cut the mouth bloody. Although some hammer headed types, mostly stallions, can't be controlled without them. It it comes to that, the horse goes down the road."

"Speaking of treatment of horses, Dad," James said. "I did some research on dosing horses. Charlie was guessing on how much venom to inject the horses with. He killed one. Then he reduced the dose. When the five we have now were staggering around on the highway down toward Shelby, they were still overdosed. So, he guessed and reduced it again. Through trial and error, he got it down to where he was only moderately overdosing the horses.

"The dose has to match the size of the horse. I've got that figured out. Charlie also doesn't keep records, so he was trusting his memory to figure out the doses. Minnie is keeping records now, so we don't screw up the dosing. I don't want to bitch, Dad. But Charlie just flies by the seat of his pants."

Yellowhenry laughed, "I could have told you that a long time ago, James. Minnie is convinced that the serpentarium will belong to you when you finish high school. You'll make a lot of money, too."

"I can see that," James said. "I enjoy my work out there, but I don't get paid for it."

"Really?" Yellowhenry frowned. "Well, that's going to change."

"It's okay, Dad. I'm just OJT right now."

"No son, that's what it's been. Now it's going to change."

Chapter 35

Then it happened. Everyone had gone home from the Greasewood Serpentarium except for Charlie who lived in the small apartment that had been added as a part of the improvements. He liked to have two or three domesticated rattlers in the apartment so he'd have companions to talk to. He also enjoyed having mush as part of his dinner because his snakes liked it, too. They would either wrap the wooden table legs of his kitchen table so their heads were next to the bowl or crawl up on the table itself.

Charlie would feed them mush with his own spoon. There was a procedure, however. He would take a bite, then give, in order, each snake a bite. If a snake tried to grab another snake's bite, he would rap it sharply on the nose with his spoon, causing it to pull back. They always rattled, but for some reason he couldn't explain, didn't strike.

He had a penchant for big rattlers, like Bo, his prized five footer that had crawled under the passenger side rocker arm panels in Captain Yellowhenry's police cruiser. Bo had perished there, and Charlie had been working ever since to get another big one tamed.

He thought he had her. The snake was a mature heavy bodied female a little over five feet long. Her disposition was sweet and calm, almost like a pet corn snake. He named her Sylvie, and he had been grooming her for months and decided to bring her into the apartment to see how she would behave in a more open and free environment. At first, she was nervous and took up refuge under his couch where she rattled a warning whenever he walked by. He ignored her and patiently waited until she came crawling out on her own. He stood in place without moving, so she could get her bearings.

She began exploring, rattling a bit whenever she encountered any of the other three snakes in the apartment. He left all the interior doors open, so she had free rein. When mush time came, she was nowhere to be seen. Soon, he had three wedge headed rattlers with their heads poised closely around the big aluminum mush bowl he used to dish out the treat every night. Each of the snakes was named in alphabetical order. Albert was a smallish three foot male that always crawled fully onto the table.

He was a polite and patient fellow who had never had his nose smacked. Bert was a four foot male that entwined the table leg. His stance was off Charlie's right elbow, so he had to be fed left handed. Carl was a beefy four foot female that crawled up the left side table leg and onto the table.

Charlie began with his first spoonful. He liked to tease the rattlers by making a big scene about how great the mush tasted. Then, he'd dip into the bowl and give his snakes, in strict alphabetical order, a spoonful apiece. The fourth was another bite for himself.

It was when he was retrieving the spoon from Bert's third scoop, that Sylvie came ploughing across the table and grabbed at the spoon. Without thinking, Charlie quickly smacked her nose. Her reaction was too swift for even someone like Charlie to avoid. She struck him in the face just below his left eye and hung on as he shrieked and pitched over backward in his chair, kicking the table with his feet, as the big female hung on emptying her venom glands into his cheek.

"No Sylvie!" he screamed, finally tearing her loose and throwing her away under the table. His thrashing as he pitched over backward, alarmed Bert. He unwound from the table leg and dropped to the floor where he coiled into the elevated striking pose of angry rattlesnakes. Charlie scrambled to his feet and Bert struck catching his right forearm just above the wrist joint.

Charlie sent Bert sailing with one whip of his arm before he stumbled to the door leading down to the clinic and the refrigerator where the antivenin was stored. He left the door to the apartment ajar. In the clinic, he injected himself with his own dose, plus the dose labeled for Minnie. A quick phone call to the hospital to report that he'd been bitten preceded his mad dash into Havre in his old beater of a pickup. He carried James' dose of antivenin with him.

So quickly did he leave that he left the outside door to the clinic open wide. The three smaller snakes from the apartment came slithering down the stairs to discover their freedom. The big female coiled up under the table and settled down. The three escapees, however, crawled, into thirty-eight degree weather. The best the three could do was to crawl into sagebrush for cover. None found rodent holes they could crawl into for shelter.

Charlie injected himself with James' dose in the Emergency bay at the hospital. He explained to the staff what had happened and what he'd done with antivenin. Then he demanded that Joe Yellowhenry be called and told what had happened. After that he collapsed.

Amy took the call in the kitchen at 9:30 that night. After getting all the information, she hurried back into the bedroom and shook Joe, who had just gone to sleep. "Honey," she said in answer to his 'Wha?", "Charlie's been bitten. He's in the hospital."

He sat bolt upright. "I knew it was gonna happen if he kept screwin' around with his goddamned pets," he shouted. He sat still in thought for a moment. "Ames," he said. "Running to the hospital won't accomplish anything tonight. We've got to run out and make sure the clinic is secure. Get James up while I dress. I'm taking my service belt in case I have to shoot some snakes."

Chapter 36

When Yellowhenry and his son pulled into the yard at the serpentarium, James exclaimed, "The door is wide open, Dad. I'll bet Charlie's pets crawled out."

"How many does he have?"

"Four if he pulled in a big female he is fond of."

"Then let's take a quick look around before we go inside," Yellowhenry said. "Go close the door and I'll start over here on my side."

James took a quick look inside the facility and heaved a sigh of relief when he saw that it wasn't alive with crawling escaped snakes. Then, he hustled out to look into the sagebrush that surrounded the site. "I found two," Yellowhenry hollered, "Where do you want them?"

James was amazed as his father came striding through the brush with a pair of rattlers coiled up around his arm like a pair of hoops. "What's with the snakes?" James asked.

"They're so cold they can't move."

"Damn," James laughed. "That makes it easy. Bring 'em into the back line next to the wall. That's where Charlie keeps 'em when he isn't fooling around with them."

"Fooling is about right," Yellowhenry said. "I told him not to keep handling these damned things barehanded."

"He's done it so long, he doesn't listen to anyone, Dad. Did you find a big heavy bodied one?"

"No. They're hard to make out because they won't rattle."

When the pair of snakes were deposited into their glassed in cages, James said, "This one hit Charlie, Dad."

"How can you tell?"

"His venom glands are partially expressed."

"Charlie must have taken another bite, then. The hospital said he'd dosed himself three times and still collapsed. Doesn't seem like one bite from that snake would be enough to do that."

"That big female could have gotten him," James said. "She was due to be milked, so her bags were full. Did they say where he was bitten?"

"Arm and face."

"Face?" James exclaimed.

"Yeah, that's what Mom said. She took the call from the hospital."

"Dad, that could kill Charlie even with antivenin shots right away."

"I'm sorry, Son. Let's finish up here and head for the hospital."

Yellowhenry noticed the open door to the apartment, he also saw that the lights in the apartment were on. His tramp on the step alerted the big female and she rattled a warning. He took a quick look around and spotted her coiled in the S shape from which strikes were projected. "James!" he shouted. "That big female is up here."

James joined his father and the pair looked at the threatening posture of the snake under the table. "How the hell do you handle a snake like that?" Yellowhenry asked.

"We'll pull on snake boots and I'll jerk her out of there with a hook so you can grab her with tongs. Then, I'll pin her head. From there, it's easy. I'll carry her back down and put her in her box."

The capture of the big reptile wasn't as easy as it sounded. Yellowhenry was the subject of a strike to his right leg boot just under his knee. The sound was that of a boxer hitting a heavy bag. The strike felt like a hammer blow. He squealed and leaped to stand on the seat of a dining room chair. James found it hilarious. "Dad, she can't bite through those boots," he laughed. "You could have grabbed her just then. She was all stretched out."

"James, if she stretches out like that at me again, she'll never do it again. I'll blow her damned head off," Yellowhenry retorted.

The snake had recoiled and tucked her head under her coils and James took the opportunity to press her head to the floor with the head of the snake hook he had in his left hand. He quickly seized her with his right hand in the three finger grip used for milking. He lifted her gently and clamped her wildly twisting body under his right arm. He tossed the hook aside and pulled her around to where he could use his left arm to support her. She began to relent with her attempts to coil. "There we go, Dad," James called happily. "She's gonna be just fine. She is the one that got Charlie in the face, though. Her venom glands are flat. She also broke off a fang."

"Will she grow it back?"

"Yeah. But it takes so long, we'll probably steak her out, tan the skin, and make a belt."

They looked for the fourth snake unsuccessfully for twenty minutes. "To hell with it, Dad," James said. "Let's go see about Charlie."

Chapter 37

When the father/son team arrived at the hospital, Charlie was asleep. "What are his chances for survival?" Yellowhenry asked.

The doctor in charge, Dr. Harvey Goetz, replied, "Quite good, actually. Mr. Goodwoman is nearly immune to snakebite. It appears he has been injecting himself with very small doses of venom over quite a long period of time. In addition to the three doses of antivenin he gave himself, we supplemented with an additional injection. Quite frankly, if it hadn't been for the bite to the face, it is likely that we wouldn't have needed to add the injection at all. We did so just to be on the safe side."

"Let's go home, James," Yellowhenry said. "Charlie is going to get a better night's sleep than we are."

"I'm going to see if we can draw blood from Charlie and sell it," James hooted.

Winter worried its way into Spring and in late April, Carolyn Malone was sponsoring a branding workshop on her Bar H7 Ranch. It was a weekend affair with the branding taking place on both Saturday and Sunday. The bunkhouse was open to anyone who wanted to stay overnight following the barbeque on Saturday night. Yellowhenry had finally bought a two horse trailer, so he loaded up Hi Boy and Pal.

James worked ahead at the serpentarium so he could get the weekend off. Yellowhenry and his son left early Saturday morning to get there in time to help with the gather. Altogether, there were ninety-eight calves to process. Yellowhenry took the lead on setting up the crew. One of the neighbors, Nolan Warren, who had two burly high school sons, Jacob and Wesley, volunteered their help to work the squeeze chute. Jacob loaded the calves into the narrow fence that led to the chute. As soon as the calves darted ahead, Wesley would slam the swinging side of the chute shut on the necks of the terrified Hereford calves. Then he kicked a trip which laid the chute over so the animals lay on their sides.

Carolyn handled the vaccination and doping of the horn buds, Yellowhenry did the branding and castration. The testicles were tossed into a bucket so they could be added to the barbecue at the end of the day. James crunched the ear tags in place and recorded the date, tag number and mother cow ear tag numbers along with the vaccination information into a branding book.

It took about ten minutes to load and unload each calf. The crew knocked off at four o'clock on Saturday so everyone could clean up in the bunkhouse and participate in the barbeque. Carolyn's nanny, Betty Jonas, had been preparing the side dishes all afternoon, so Yellowhenry's donning the chef's hat and laying the steaks and testicles on the big charcoal grill was the final step to setting the table for the party of twelve, including Carolyn's triplets. Ice cream in round two gallon drums finished off the spread.

All hands stayed overnight, with James and the Warren brothers throwing bedrolls in the bunkhouse. Yellowhenry was given the same bedroom on the second floor of the ranch house as he'd had the night Roy Malone had been killed by a grizzly bear several years earlier. It was just after midnight when Carolyn slipped into the room to find him sitting on the bed, gazing out at the cattle still to be run through the branding regimen.

"I was thinking maybe you'd come to see me," he said as she sat down beside him. She was wearing house slippers and a bathrobe. He was sitting in his boxers.

"Joe," she began. "I had the strangest conversation with Amy."

"Let me guess," he said, glancing sideways at her. "She wants us to get married after she's gone?"

"Yes. She also knows."

"How the hell do you women know when us men screw someone else? Can you answer that?"

"Yes. I'm an expert. Remember, my husband could not keep it in his pants. It's almost like a smell. Guilt radiates like odor, Joe. Not just from men either. Amy had me pegged like a frog on a needle. I felt like such a shit. She is looking way beyond that, though. She is thinking of her kids and you. I don't know, however, where you are, Joe. Can you tell me?"

"Yes. I am deeply and madly in love with Amy right now, Carolyn. Maybe it's a just an act of contrition. I don't know and don't really care. Hell, Carolyn, we have sex once or twice a month, and we use dental dams because of her cancer. And I love it. If I lose Amy, you need to know I can't give you children."

"I know. Amy and I are like sisters. She told me about your vasectomy. Joe, if we get together, won't ten kids be enough?" she chuckled.

"I guess I finally did something right," he said.

"Oh, Joe," she said. "don't say finally. You do things right all the time."

"Doesn't seem like it."

"Amy knows something else, too."

"Damnit," he said.

"Yeah, damnit, Joe. Not just from Amy, either. You and Flora Lightenger in Glasgow."

"How did that come out?"

"Well, honey," she said, "packing the woman piggyback along the highway with cell phone shutterbugs passing by as she was trying her darndest to give you a hickey, wasn't exactly discreet. You know, film at eleven?"

"So, someone showed her a snapshot, I suppose."

"I don't know who, or even if she actually saw it, but she knows. Damn you, Joe. You cheated on both of us, you know."

"Christ, Carolyn. I can't remember the last time I did anything right when it comes to women. Amy hasn't said anything about it to me, though."

"Joe, she won't, but it brought up something else. She's afraid that you'll remember it and go back for more." Carolyn shrugged the robe down off her naked shoulders.

He turned and slid away from her, lifting his right knee up between them. "What are you doing?" he said, alarmed.

"I've been instructed to try and make love to you again, Joe. Amy wants you to be assured that I'll be the woman you want after she's gone," Carolyn said, tears choking her voice. "Just say no and I'll go."

The robe had slipped to her waist and her breasts were fully nippled as her shoulders shook. He looked past her and into the future, hesitating and uncertain. Then he reached for her and they kissed.

Chapter 38

Yellowhenry and Amy continued with their dedication to each other cemented by their children and the fear that their time together was being truncated by her disease. Neither mentioned the tryst that Carolyn and he had consummated at the branding of her cattle.

James went through a growth spurt that spring and summer. He turned fourteen in August. In a family tradition, he stood with his back to the measuring wall in the family kitchen. He had gained three inches of height and stood five feet ten inches tall. He'd also gained fifteen more pounds. Great excitement was building as James looked forward to the high school rodeo season which began in the fall and ended with the finals in late spring.

His work at the serpentarium had become paid after Minnie and Yellowhenry had a discussion about child labor laws. "Joe," Minnie had laughed. "I've been laying his money aside in a special account for him. If you want him to have it, I'll give it to him today."

"How much are we talking?" he'd asked.

"A little over ten thousand."

"Jesus," he exclaimed like he'd been rammed in the ass with a hot poker. "I was thinking minimum wage, Minnie."

"You poor, poor man," she'd giggled. "I told you the kid would be making a half a million a year when he takes over. You don't get it. Do you know what an antivenin shot runs at the vet's for a dog that's been snakebit?"

"Well, no. I can't say as I've ever asked."

"Seventeen hundred, Joe. We're dealing in very expensive products here."

"Don't tell me what the kid's time is worth. I don't want to be tempted to take up snake wrangling. Just pay him minimum wages and continue to bank the rest of it."

"What about Susie?" she'd asked.

"I don't want to know. I'll trust you to do the right thing."

Charlie Goodwoman had spent the night in the hospital and half the next day. Not because of the massive injection of snake venom he'd suffered, but because his face had to be sutured where Sylvie had bitten him. A fang had to be extracted and the punctures opened and drained. When he walked into the clinic the next afternoon and asked where Sylvie was, Minnie slid the side of her hand across her throat. "She didn't go to waste, Charlie."

"You mean she's gone already? Damnit, Minnie. She was just coming around to being nice and gentle," he wailed.

"Those other three?" she grinned ghoulishly. "Shlish, shlash. One got away out in the brush, though. Maybe you can find him. We couldn't."

He scoured the brush for his pet, but no sign of the snake was ever discovered. Charlie finally quit trying to make pets out of rattlesnakes. He got a border collie, instead. The dog was three years old when he got her. Ironically, the sheepherder the dog came from had died of snakebite. The dog, that Charlie named Sylvie, had no fear of snakes. She'd learned while herding sheep to leave them alone. Charlie found her much better company than his snakes. He showed his love by giving her tiny injections of snake venom.

With school back in session, James turned out for the Havre High School Blue Ponies rodeo team. He discovered right away that he couldn't be a one event participant. Since he owned his own horse, he and a sophomore girl, Cindy Chattsworth, who also owned her own horse, became team ropers. They also became boyfriend/girlfriend. Her mother put her on birth control pills as soon as she saw them rope together, hold hands, and kiss passionately. "Mom, he's only fourteen, for heaven's sake," Cindy had protested.

"I'm not worried about him," her mother had said.

The bucking horses available for the Blue Ponies were, by and large, those contracted for the rodeos. There were rarely any horses available for practice. For most of the participants, it was, 'Grab your bucking rope and hang on.' James stood out immediately as a natural. So good was he, that students who had never paid any attention to the rodeo team started showing up at the rodeo grounds, just to watch him.

When the last of the outdoor events in late October was scheduled for Havre, he drew a saddle bronc horse that had never been ridden. The stir around the bucking chute was audible. James knew nothing of the horse and the stock contractor told him nothing, either. The horse was a big powerful all black stallion named Black Soot Thunder.

When the chute gate opened the horse reared out and came down on his front legs in a bone rattling leg plant, followed by a straight up leap coupled to a near vertical rear leg kick. When he hit the ground he changed directions and leaped skyward again. Every move was accented by a heavy grunt. James seemed to know just what the roadmap of the big stallion was, and he spurred the entire ride raking the horse from his shoulders to his flanks. When the ride ended, the pickup men were reluctant to get too close to the stallion as he continued to buck. One of them finally pulled the flanking strap and the big black began running flat out. James looked for help, and finding none, jumped off, hit the ground running, and did a flip in the air, ending with him running a few more steps before he stopped. Then, he unsnapped his chaps legs and walked back to the chutes.

The applause was uniform and sustained as he was congratulated by competitors from all other eight attending schools. The Havre High School spectators were loud and boisterous. When it was announced that he had set a new state high school record for saddle bronc riding with a score of ninety-five, the Blue Ponies supporters doubled their volume. A small group of adults seated in the bleachers applauded modestly. Yellowhenry, Amy, Carolyn, Susie and Charlie were awestruck. "I told you, Ames," Yellowhenry said proudly. "I knew he was gifted when he took on Pal. He was grinnin' through the whole thing, and I can tell you, Pal would have dumped me in five seconds."

Chapter 39

Carolyn decided to sell her ranch. She didn't want to be a homeschool mother to her triplets and she enjoyed less and less being isolated for long periods of time on her ranch. While her nanny, Betty Jonas, was a comfort, she craved the company of people her own age. After selling off her calf crop in October, she put the ranch on the market.

Amy was pleased when Carolyn made the announcement. In the back of her mind, she heard a piece of her plan fall into place. It made her happy.

Yellowhenry ferried Amy back and forth to Billings once a month for treatment for her cervical cancer. Blasingame had referred her to an oncologist, Dr. Shirley Marpham. The initial treatment was a regimen of chemotherapy which made Amy lose her hair. She wore wigs and wept incessantly during the process of having mats and handsful of her hair simply give up their grip on her scalp. She dutifully tended to her children, but she eventually suspended her husband's conjugal privileges. "I just can't do it to go through the motions, honey," she said. "I hope you understand."

"I get it. It's okay. When you get better," he said and smiled.

She didn't believe him and braced herself for his occasional liaisons, she hoped, with Carolyn. The accompanying illness cast her into dark studies from which nothing stirred her except the screams of her children. Her housekeeping, which had always been a source of pride for her, fell into disrepair.

Without being asked, Minnie stepped in and took over. She spent as much time at the Yellowhenry's as she did at her own place or the serpentarium. She did her bookkeeping and marketing for the clinic more at Amy's than she did at home.

Following the chemotherapy, came radiation treatments. It was between Thanksgiving and Christmas that Dr. Marpham spoke to Yellowhenry privately. "Your wife is not doing well," she began. "Not because the treatment is ineffective, either. Mr. Yellowhenry, she just doesn't want to live. We'll be finished with radiation before Christmas, but I think in the best interests of your family, you should be aware that your wife is showing suicidal tendencies."

"I know," Yellowhenry said. "I see it, too. I just don't think there's any way to stop her."

"There is counseling."

"Not in Havre. And she won't go anywhere else for it. I've suggested it. Hell, she won't leave the house to go grocery shopping."

"Well, I wish you well, sir. Let me know if there's anything I can do to help."

Carolyn's ranch sold in early December. Since she'd owned it free and clear, she had no need for an income, but she took a job in a department store in Havre just to have something to do. It became apparent very soon that she had a special way with dealing with people looking to buy clothing. Sales in the clothing department went up by 25% in the first two weeks of her tenure.

She rented a four bedroom house, much to Betty's relief. "I was so afraid you were going to let me go," she said.

"Betty," Carolyn had exclaimed. "I'm shocked that you'd think I'd ever cast adrift the only gramma my kids have ever really known."

Betty broke down in tears. "Thank you, Carolyn. I secretly feel that way about your children. I'm so relieved you think so, too."

Carolyn did her best to cheer Amy up and sat with her as often as she could. It didn't seem to help. While she didn't stop completely, her visits became more and more infrequent. Amy didn't appear to notice. With Carolyn living in town, another part of Amy's grand plan had dropped into place.

As time had gone on, Amy had not only lost her hair, she had also lost an alarming amount of weight. Yellowhenry had come to accept that he'd lost her. He stood by her nonetheless. Even with Carolyn in town and available to him, he did not avail himself of her.

Christmas was torture for him. He knew he'd never experience another with her. Nevertheless, he endured with a stiff upper lip. Amy gave away her gifts to her children. Susie who had grown tall for a twelve year old girl could wear her mother's clothes. She didn't understand when her mother passed her a filmy red nightie she had received from Yellowhenry. He'd bought it at Carolyn's suggestion that it might brighten her moods when she wore it. "You save this for your wedding night, sweetie," Amy had whispered to her daughter. "You'll see why, and you can laugh with your mother."

The following day, Susie asked Yellowhenry, "What's with Mom? Giving her Christmas gifts away. It's like she doesn't think she's gonna live."

"Her cancer treatment is doing that to her. Once she gets that behind her, she'll be okay," he assured her. Secretly he feared the worst.

Chapter 40

In an odd twist of events, Yellowhenry ran into Flora Lightenger shortly after the New Year. Charlie was envenomating his dog, Sylvie, with tiny injections. As usual, Charlie was guessing and he overdid it. His pet needed a vet. His old beater of a pickup wouldn't start, so he called Yellowhenry. It was midafternoon, so Yellowhenry had adequate time to drive out, pick up Charlie and the dog, and make it to the clinic before it shut down.

Flora signed them up and checked them in. They happened to be the only clients in the clinic at that moment. Charlie and Sylvie were led into the inner chambers while Yellowhenry browsed around out front. Flora returned and flew at him reaching to embrace him. He caught her upper arms and held her off. "I can't, Flora," he said firmly. "My wife is fighting cancer and it doesn't look good. So, please, if you will."

She stepped back and looked at him. What she saw was a man who had aged years since their tryst in Glasgow. "I'm so sorry, Joe. I can tell this has been a strain on you. If there's anything I can do, I'm here every day. Just call, Joe. I'm a good listener."

He smiled grimly, "Careful, Flora. I'm going to need all the friends I can get."

"I want to be one of those. I'll get someone to help Charlie."

As it happened, the dog needed to be held overnight, so Yellowhenry drove Charlie back to the serpentarium. "I'll pick Sylvie up tomorrow afternoon and bring her out."

It was late when he called on the Hill County Veterinary Clinic the following afternoon. Sylvie was still suffering, but Charlie had called and demanded she be released. Flora volunteered to ride out and hold the dog in the backseat. "So, how are you and your daughters doing, Flora?" Yellowhenry asked.

"Terrific, Joe, in most ways," she answered.

"Something with the kids at school?"

"No. You."

"I hope this isn't related to our one night stand," he said.

"Well, of course not, Joe. It's because we haven't gone swimmin' lately."

He found himself laughing. "All righty, then, Flora. Let's do the Polar Bear Plunge this weekend."

"Just my luck," she retorted. "From the heat of passion to freezing my balls off. That's the way it's been ever since Glasgow."

They drove in silence for a few miles before he commented. "Damn, Flora, that felt good."

"I take it laughs have been sorta rare, lately."

"Nonexistent."

"Well, I'm not gonna turn into a clown for you. But I'm glad we found something to laugh about."

Shortly after, they pulled into the serpentarium. Yellowhenry parked and walked around to take Sylvie in his arms. "I've got her," Flora said, stepping out and picking the limp form from the seat. "Just show me where to take her."

"All right," he said. "Have you been in here before?"

"No. Heard of it is all."

"Okay, then," he said slowly. "Step right this way. There's a staircase dead ahead from the door. Leads up to an apartment. Dog will go up there."

He swept the door open and stood aside. The scene was startling both auditorily and visually. As soon as the door opened, snakes started rattling. It was a shock to all first time visitors akin to what happens to first timers when they step onto the kill floor of a slaughterhouse. Shock bordering on the sense of rising gorge. A snake bullpen, of sorts, was set off to the left in the center of a long enclosed lean-to. The rattling emanated from there. A snake milking station was set in the center of the main floor. Charlie was standing there stroking the glands of a furiously rattling four foot snake. He looked over his shoulder and called, "I'll be right up."

"Oh, shit!" Flora blurted. She hustled to the staircase and darted to the top.

"Hold on, Flora!" Yellowhenry shouted. "I'll get the door up there."

He pulled the entry door closed and took the stairs two at a time. He cautiously opened the upper door, reached along the wall, and flipped a light switch. A riotous rattling was set off instantly. Yellowhenry spotted a pair of rattlers that were setting off for hiding places. He pulled the door closed and shouted for Charlie. Then, he said, "We'll be just a minute, Flora. Let me hold Sylvie."

When he gathered the dog into his arms and lifted, he boosted Flora's breasts unintentionally. A flash of heat struck them both and they looked into each other's eyes. "Sorry," he said.

"I'm not," she grinned.

"What's up?" Charlie said coming up the stairs.

"There are snakes in your apartment," Yellowhenry said. "I thought you were through with trying to make pets out of rattlers."

"I am. Those will be wild ones."

"How would they get in here, Charlie?"

"Chasing mice, Joe. We have mice all over this place because, as you know, we feed them to snakes and some of the mice get away. Well, they breed if the wild ones don't get 'em first. Gives the wild ones a constant food supply. These are the last two of the wild ones, though. The rest are denned up. I keep these two around to act as mousers."

"So, what are you going to do with those in there, now?"

"I have a pair of snake tongs behind the door. Let me get by you and I'll clear the snakes out. You can come on in. They always take off away from the door."

"Aren't you afraid of stepping on one?" Flora shuddered.

"Naw. That's why I wear snake boots."

Twenty minutes later, with his mousers stashed in the snake bull pen, the trio was looking over the still limp border collie. "We gave her fluids intravenously last night and today, Charlie," Flora said. "Dr. Arbordooven says if she doesn't come out of it tonight, she never will."

"Jesus Christ, Charlie," Yellowhenry demanded. "How did you calculate the dose you gave her, for God's sake?"

"Well, I took a horse dose and cut it way down. I admit it was a bigger shot than what she'd been getting, but I figured she had some immunity already built up."

"How often did you envenomate her?"

"Every five or six weeks."

"You mean you didn't keep a chart?"

"Hell no. I kept it in my head," Charlie said defensively. "So what?"

"I'll tell you, 'So what,'" Yellowhenry said, getting angry. "It's called cruelty to animals. You've done it before. Hell, you killed a horse, and over doped five others. Now you've, perhaps, added a dog. I can't keep overlooking that, Charlie. It's the goddamned law," Yellowhenry yelled. "If this dog dies, I'm going to report it so that I don't get blamed for negligence in allowing an ongoing dangerous practice to animals to just keep going on and on right under my nose. Do you get it?"

"Yeah," Charlie said, hanging his head. "I should have asked James to help me out. He keeps everything charted and balanced and ratioed out. I just never got into that."

"Well, get into it now. And quit trying to envenomate every damned thing you find. Save it for yourself. I'll keep my fingers crossed for Sylvie. Come on Flora, I'll run you back to the vet's."

When the pair reached the car, Flora caught Yellowhenry's arm and turned him to her. Before he could back away, she had him pinned against the side of his cruiser. "Kiss me, Joe," she breathed. "We both need it. You more than me."

"Flora, this is not the time or the place."

"It's dark. We're in the middle of nowhere, and we won't take more than five minutes."

He tried to protest, but her kiss smothered that. Then, before he could stop, he was inside her as he crouched and leaned back against the cruiser door while she did him.

Chapter 41

For the next month, Yellowhenry berated himself at times nearly every day. He purposely stayed away from Flora. He couldn't understand what it was about her, that whenever he spent any amount of time with her, they fornicated. Two for two. The load of guilt he felt from that made him a bear to be around at work. He felt like he was no better than a male whore. Another Roy Malone. His relief for it was to take a field trip to Helena for a gathering of law enforcement officials, who were there to collaborate with a growing epidemic of drug abuse all across the state. It was a three day conference for which his office, because of his absence, was grateful.

Not much came of it. Yellowhenry thought it weird that a meeting of that sort arrived at the conclusion that maintaining the status quo was as much as Montana law could be expected to do. The real problem was a system of lax federal enforcement on the southern border. In his experience, when a committee met, change was the order of the day. Otherwise, what was the need for a committee?

Then, on the way back, Yellowhenry pulled into the Cascade Mountains Café in Cascade just at closing time. As soon as he walked in the door, Monti Collier saw him. "Ah, ha!" she exclaimed. "A perfect Joe for a perfect cup of Joe."

He looked around, "I could use a cup to go, Monti. I see you're getting ready to close up."

"I am. I'll be just a minute, then I want to talk to you about an idea I have."

"Okay," he said setting his Stetson on a table and sitting down. She bustled around, locking the door, flipping the 'open' sign to 'closed', and turning off external lights. Then as she'd done before, she grabbed two coffee cups and a coffee pot. "Come on," she said. "Let's go upstairs so we aren't disturbed by someone pounding on the door because they spot us through the cracks."

"All right, Monti," he said, "but no see through nightie this time."

"No problem," she agreed.

At her kitchen table she laid out what she had in mind. "Cascade is just too small and too near Great Falls for me to get any real traction in the restaurant business, Joe. I copyrighted, 'Trooper Joe says try our perfect cup of Joe.'"

"You did?"

"Yes! It's my perfect calling card. I want to take it to my new Cascade Mountains Restaurant in Havre."

"In Havre?" he said in surprise and disbelief. "Why there?"

"Because you're there. Don't you see? Right where you are most famous is where my logo will work best. I already have a spot for a restaurant picked out thanks to my silent partner. But I want to make sure it's okay with you. I was even planning a field trip up there to talk to you about it, and in you walk. It's like an omen," she said, pleased with her luck.

"Well, I won't guarantee traction, but if you want to go for it, go ahead," he smiled.

"Wonderful," she beamed. "I'm so delighted. Thank you, Joe." By then they were seated side by side on her living room sofa. She poured coffee topping off his cup.

"Whoa, Monti," he laughed. "You'll have me watering the bushes every ten minutes between here and Havre."

Her laugh floated back to him from a short hallway leading to her bathroom. "Talk about watering!"

He chuckled to himself and took the top off his coffee. He set the cup down on a doily on her coffee table, lifted his legs onto the table, and leaned back against the sofa-back and closed his eyes. A few minutes later he heard her returning and opened his eyes. She wasn't wearing a nightie.

Later, as they lay naked in her bed, nearly spent, he asked out of curiosity. "Is your silent partner anyone I'd know?"

"It's sort of unusual, but maybe. My partner is a woman. A rancher's widow by the name of Carolyn Malone."

Yellowhenry, who had been regaining his erection, suddenly went limp and dead quiet. "Do you know her, Joe?" Monti asked sensing the sudden change in his demeanor and posture.

"Well, yes. I do know Carolyn. You couldn't have a better silent partner then Carolyn."

Without too much more injury inflicted upon himself, Yellowhenry extricated himself a half hour later and set out for Havre. He was completely bewildered. Nevertheless, he drove through the night. At three o'clock in the morning, he pulled into his home and as silently as he could, crawled onto the sofa and went to sleep in his uniform.

Chapter 42

In late February, Amy passed away in her home. Yellowhenry was by her side, holding her in his arms. He knew her time had come and he pleaded for her to fight it. She whispered, "I've always loved you, Joe. I forgive you for what I know you've done and for what you've done that I don't know about."

She smiled as he kissed her. "I'm so sorry, Amy," he sobbed.

"There's something else, Joe," she said so softly it was more breath than whisper. "Please forgive me, too. And marry Carolyn as soon as you can for our kids' sake." Then, she took one last deep breath that she released along with her life.

Two months later, Yellowhenry was in a confessional conversation with Art McClintock. He was laying bare his soul. "Amy had it all set up for you and Carolyn, but you had relations with Flora and Monti. Is that right?" Art asked.

"Yes. I've not only cheated on Amy, I've cheated on Carolyn, too."

"Well, that's a noble sentiment, Joe," Art said, "but how do you figure you cheated on a woman you aren't even engaged to, much less married to?"

"It's just the way things are. Amy set this whole thing up with Carolyn. She's the chosen one."

"Okay, but if that's so, you've already cheated on her, too. Twice with one woman and once with a different woman. It may be that Carolyn is the next woman for you, but not until she is. Right now you shouldn't be committed to any of those women. Then, since in reality, you would be just like any other bachelor, your affairs and one night stands with women you date are not betrayals of anyone. I wouldn't marry any of those women, and I sure as hell wouldn't think that every piece of ass I got was cheating on one of them."

The sense that Yellowhenry got was that if he didn't commit to any of the three women, he couldn't be held, even in his own mind, as cheating on them. It was a vast relief. He still upbraided himself from time to time for breaking his marriage vows. It slanted his view of his relationship with all three of the women who had intersected his sexual orbit. To their credit, none of them pushed their plight.

Besides, he had bigger fish to fry, anyway. He discovered very quickly what single working moms had to do on a daily basis. He felt like a one legged man in a butt kicking contest. He leaned on Minnie until she quit, saying, "Hire a nanny or marry Carolyn. I'm tired of being dry humped by your personal circumstances every damned day."

His first gambit was to sidle into the new restaurant in town. The Cascade Mountains Restaurant was painted with the same motif as its predecessor. It was not, however, a one woman café. The wait staff of three shifts of a maître d', kitchen staff, three waitresses, and two bus boys were not as successful in parlaying the mountain paintings into the tips Monti had enjoyed in Cascade. The perfect cup of Joe worked better. Monti was also tied up, managing the bar and kitchen. The place opened at six in the morning and closed at midnight. She just didn't have time or energy to share their perfect cups.

Yellowhenry slipped in for coffee and unexpectedly bumped into Carolyn, who was doing an audit of procedures, courtesy, and efficiency. She spotted him sitting at a booth alone and unobtrusively looking around. He half rose when she slid in opposite him. "Carolyn," he smiled. "This place becomes you."

She laughed ruefully, "This place is more frustrating than you are, Joe."

"Well, that's partially right. I'm frustrated," he said.

"Let me guess," she said. "You are having a hell of a time being both Mom and Dad?"

"I don't know how you women do it," he exclaimed. "Day care, kindergarten, elementary school, high school, and a job, too, besides running a household! For Chrissakes, it's unbelievable. If I didn't have James, Susie, and Minnie to help with it all, I couldn't do it. And now Minnie's given me the middle finger."

She laughed pleasantly and reached across the table to pat his hand. "You need a nanny and housekeeper. Do you want me to help you look?"

"What are you and Betty doing in your spare time," he grinned. "How'd you like to get married?"

"With this place, I'd never have time to be a wife, Joe," she laughed. "Besides you have some sand in your shoes along with Monti and Flora to get shaken out before I'd ever venture back into those waters."

He felt his face flush and he looked at her closely. "You know?"

"Did you think you had them sworn to secrecy?" she asked, somewhat puzzled.

"I guess I just figured they'd want it that way. It never came up, really."

"My dear," she said, "life goes on. Amy knew that and she knew about you and me. When she got sick, she began planning your future with me. What she hoped for was a smooth transition from her to me without giving much thought to my hopes, desires, and ambitions. She took love for granted. Believed that if everything else was in place, love could be learned."

"That's funny," he chuckled. "She told me that, too, before we were married."

"I admit that I've given serious thought to life with you, Joe. And maybe somewhere down the line, if you are still of a mind and have shaken loose from your women, I could see us getting properly engaged with marriage to follow. Don't forget, I've already had one man who couldn't dedicate himself to my bed."

"Carolyn," he protested, "I'm not really like that."

"Yes you are, Joe. All three of us women came after you and you took us. Not your fault in that sense of it, but you, like Roy, are a chick magnet. Now that you are a widower, chicks will be even more available. What you need right now is a nanny and housekeeper. Or, a wife. Flora might marry you if you'd ask. At one time, anyway, she would have happily quit her job to do it. She still might. You'll have to check it out. Monti is just too busy with this place."

"And you are out?" he asked sadly.

"Yes, Joe," she said. "Never a wife, but always a friend."

Chapter 43

The housekeeper and cook turned out to be a man referred to Yellowhenry by Minnie who had heard about him at the community center on the reservation. Russel Thistle was a boon to the Yellowhenry household. He was a Native American who had spent his fifty-seven years of life on Indian reservations. He had been a healthcare worker with a restless spirit. Woman friendly but never married, his four liaisons had produced nine children, which his partners raised without him. None demanded anything of him, but whenever his fortunes allowed, he sent generous sums of money to them.

Yellowhenry threw together a small apartment for him in the loft of the barn and stable. Thistle, who was willing to work hard and cheerfully without complaint, was grateful. James immediately put him to work at the serpentarium whenever his duties as housekeeper allowed. The pay was generous and Thistle happily shared with the four mothers of his children.

Yellowhenry's relief was immense. Thistle's experience with children and his never-ending cheerfulness turned a rather dour, going through the motions household into a pleasant and purposeful home. It made Yellowhenry aware that, like it or not, his house needed a woman.

He also looked at the situation practically. With seven children still in their teens and younger, the expense of maintaining the place was slowing eating away his life's savings. With a wife in the house, he could let Thistle go. So, he approached Flora. She made a lusty and willing partner, but there were four problems to overcome. Despite what Carolyn had said, she loved her job and wouldn't quit, so she wouldn't have the time required to keep the home humming. Leaving her home to live as a white bread wife on the reservation was not appealing to her, either. She was also unwilling to move her daughters from their school in Havre to the school on the reservation, and she wanted to have more children, which Yellowhenry could not provide. As a result, they became lovers of the buddy type. At the same time, Yellowhenry kept an eye open for other prospects.

Things shaped up at home in late August for Yellowhenry to take a drive, so he went east. Out of curiosity, he decided to drop in on the new owners of Carolyn Malone's ranch. As soon as he stopped, a pair of black and tan hounds came running from the barn and jumped to the side of his car, with tongues lolling as they bayed at Yellowhenry while he yelled for them to get down. "Hey! You dogs. Git offa there," came a voice from the barn. "Go on, now! Git!"

The dogs jumped down and trotted back toward the barn. The man who had yelled at them came striding across the yard as Yellowhenry opened his car door and looked at the scratch marks on his cruiser's door. "Farm and ranch dogs," he muttered. "It's like they're trained to scratch vehicle doors."

"Well, well, well," the fellow walking toward him exclaimed. "If it ain't Trooper Joe, hisself. What brings you out into this neck of the woods?"

"Just a friendly call. Are you the new owner?"

"Naw. Foreman. Jack Payne, Captain. At your service," the tall, gangly ranch hand grinned, snapping a salute.

"Joe Yellowhenry, Jack," he responded extending his hand. "Where is the owner?"

"Over to the house. His horse is a wheelchair these days. Not totally disabled, but he's down in the back. His missus and daughter take care of him. Poor bastard. Wouldn't quit trying to take the top off a rank horse. Got throwed and jammed his back. Come on, I'll take you over and you can meet Newt King and the wife, Julia, and the daughter, Julie."

"Thanks," Yellowhenry said. "How are things going here?"

"Bears are the shits. Guess that's how the woman who used to own this place lost her man. You know anything about that?"

"Some," Yellowhenry answered.

"Heard the police let the bear have at the poor bastard. Wouldn't even shoot it when they had the chance. That right?"

"It's a long story, Jack. No, that's not right, but I'm not into arguing against rumor and non-truths right now."

"You don't say. I'd like to hear the truth."

"Some other time, Jack," Yellowhenry said. "Do we knock, or are you allowed to walk in?"

"Oh, I'm allowed. Wipe your feet. Missus is right fussy about trackin' in mud and shit."

"Will do, thanks for calling your dogs down, Jack. It's been nice meetin' you."

"Don't you want me to introduce you?"

"Nope, I got 'er, Jack. Thanks just the same," Yellowhenry said, stepping into the house and closing the door on Payne's face.

He walked into the kitchen from the back door and as he removed his hat, he came face to face with a young woman who said, "There you are. I heard you talking to Jack. I'm Julie King." She extended her hand and they shook.

"Joe Yellowhenry."

"Trooper Joe," she smiled. "We didn't do it."

He grinned and returned, "They all say that."

"I'll bet. Come meet my folks."

He couldn't help but notice the modest sashay of her walk and hips as she led him into the living room. "Mama, Daddy," she said. "Meet Trooper Joe."

King made an effort to stand, but Yellowhenry waved him back and stepped to shake hands. "Joe Yellowhenry," he smiled.

"Newton King. My wife, Julia." The woman was obviously native and unusually attractive for her age.

She smiled and attempted to rise from her seat on the sofa where she was knitting a stocking cap. "That's all right," Yellowhenry said. "No need to leave your seat." A ball of yarn rolled across the floor and he stooped to catch it and cracked heads with Julie who had done the same thing. The ball rolled into a chair and stopped, neither pursuing it further as they stood rubbing their heads. "Are you all right?" he asked.

She laughed, "Oh, I'm fine. Hell of a way to make a first impression, though. I'll get Mama's yarn." She was wearing a pair of tan, soft cotton pants that tended to cling, and when she bent over, Yellowhenry felt a pulse of heat as he looked at the spread of her rump. He turned away quickly, but he also felt a sudden rush of heat to his face at the view he hadn't expected. He guessed her age at about thirty. She was obviously half native, which to Yellowhenry's eye made her a thrilling possibility. At five feet, eight inches in height and 130 pounds, all nicely distributed, everything was in place for him to really look at her face. She was stunning to him. Facially, she looked like she could be Amy's sister. He was, without any intention of looking for it, hooked.

"Joe," King asked, "can we offer you a cup of coffee?"

"I'd be grateful," he answered.

"Julie, do you mind?" King asked his daughter.

"I've got it," she replied. "Cream or sugar, Joe?"

"Black is just fine," Yellowhenry answered.

She returned to join him where he had taken a seat in a straight backed chair off to the side of the floor-to-ceiling rock fireplace. She pulled a chair over to where she could sit and share a cup of coffee with him. She did it so naturally that to Julia's eye, they just fit together.

Yellowhenry, in visiting with the family, discovered that Julia was half Pawnee. He knew that Pawnee women were often quite naturally beautiful. So was she. As they visited, the subject of the killer bear could not be avoided, so Yellowhenry told them the story. All of it. Julie was mesmerized. When she noticed that their coffee had gone cold, she retrieved the pot and poured more.

"So, that one bear killed two men," King mused.

"He did. Knocked off a fifteen hundred pound bull and came within a whisker of killing my horse. Blinded a highway patrolman in one eye, and damned near got the sheriff in a beaver pond."

"Just one mean son of a bitch," King added.

"Not really, Newt. He was just being what he was. A grizzly bear. Top of the food chain and not afraid of anything."

"How'd you feel about goin' after another one?"

"Sheriff's job, Newt. But whoever goes, he'd be wise to pack at least a .300 magnum. A .365 H&H Magnum would be even better."

"That's what I told Julie. So, there, Sis," he laughed and pointed at his daughter. "I know it kicks, but when you go for bear, so does my .300"

Chapter 44

James was scratching Sylvie's ears when she suddenly stood up and began staring at a mouse hole in a corner behind the door in Charlie's apartment. Shortly a rattlesnake poked its head and a foot of its body through before it stopped as the snake flicked its tongue testing for scent. On a whim, James pulled a pebble from his jacket pocket, stood, and fired a rocket that snapped the snake's neck four inches behind its head. The snake came slithering into the apartment where it twisted in a raucously rattling heap.

"What'd you do that for?" an incensed Charlie demanded.

"I've been practicing how my dad does that. I wanted to see if I could bag an animal. That snake was my first opportunity."

"Oh, yeah? Well, your dad gave me hell for cruelty to animals. What the hell do you call that?"

"A snake crawling into an apartment occupied by people who live and work there is called self-protection, Charlie. Don't worry about that wild one. Since they crawled out of their dens, they're all over this place," James said. "Minnie is getting spooked, Susie won't even come out anymore, and Russ has agreed with her. Your wild ones are taking over, Charlie. Hell, they're even in the hay in the barn. You know that. When you pitch down a forkful of hay, you have to shake it out to make sure there isn't a snake in it."

Charlie had gotten up and grabbed a set of snake tongs he kept behind the door. He picked up the broken necked snake, opened the door to his refrigerator, and dropped the intensely rattling snake into one of the vegetable crispers that had been altered so that it was open at the top. As he closed the refer door, he asked, "So what do you want to do about it?"

"We need to put up snake proof fencing. Then, have a snake roundup inside."

"Well, then we'll be overrun by mice," Charlie sniffed.

"Not if we leave two or three inside. Kicking a couple of the wild ones out of the way once in a while is one thing, Charlie. A half dozen twice a day is annoying."

"Have you checked out how much that'll cost us?"

"Thirty-two thousand, installed. Including the stable and barn. Minnie's checked it out," James said.

"Do we have that kind of money?"

"It will be a write off on taxes. Our bank balance last month was $150,000, gave or take a few. Yes, we have that kind of money, but if we can't keep our help, our production drops, our communication and marketing suffers. The money we make diminishes. The fence is a win/win for us, Charlie. The fencing company will be here day after tomorrow."

"For a fourteen or fifteen year old kid, you seem to be making some pretty big decisions regarding my company."

"Charlie, when we had that reorganization meeting this summer I became an equal partner with you and Minnie as soon as I turned eighteen. Remember? So, you've just been outvoted two to one."

"Well, yeah, I remember, but I didn't think you'd try to take over. Not yet, anyway."

"Just take the money we're makin' and run Charlie. That's what I'd do if I were you," James smiled.

"Ha, ha," Charlie said. "I'll take the money, but I ain't runnin' nowhere."

Yellowhenry was in the kitchen talking Julie through bear behavior while her mother was wheeling Newt to the outhouse. He was as much learning about her as he was telling her what he knew about bears. "If you do go grizzly hunting, the best advice I can give you, Julie," he said seriously, "is don't go alone and don't go with someone who is inexperienced."

"Okay," she said. "I'll go with you."

"Ha, ha, ho, ho!" he chuckled. "I get a pass on this one. The last one had his choice of which ass he wanted to take a big bite of. He left me mine. I'd like to hang onto it a while longer. So would my seven kids."

"You have seven kids?" she asked, startled.

"Yes. Five are mine. My wife had two when we were married."

"How many more do you want?" she asked.

"I can't have any more."

"Well, just for the sake of hypotheses, what if I added three more?"

"I'd have to add on to my house," he grinned.

"But, you'd do that?"

"Just for the sake of hypotheses, for you, I certainly would."

"Well, that answers a few questions about your character. I don't have any kids, but I could sure use some. I lost my husband because I couldn't produce any."

"Are we talking possibilities, here?" Yellowhenry asked.

"Mmmhmm," she smiled. "As soon as I had a good look at you."

"Well. That's mutual," he said. "So you wouldn't refuse my courting you?"

She leaned across the corner of the kitchen table and kissed him.

Chapter 45

Yellowhenry spent another hour exploring the area of the ranch headquarters, learning about the bear problem at the Bar H7. He found the track of a big boar outside the old chicken coop where Carolyn kept her flock. The Kings, however, had no chickens.

"Jack?" Yellowhenry asked. "You sleep in the bunkhouse. Don't those dogs raise hell when that bear comes around here?"

"I keep them locked in a stable, so the bear can't tangle with 'em. They're good on blacks, Captain, but a Grizz is a whole 'nother story."

"Okay, but what about you? Don't you hear anything?"

"Oh, yeah. But that old cowhand the other bear grabbed? Took him right offa the porch. I ain't about to open no doors on no griz, Captain. I got me a .3030 in case he tries to get into the bunkhouse. Then he's dead meat, by God. I'll take that son of a bitch down, he gets that close."

Yellowhenry looked at the man to see if he were serious. "Jack, I'm going to tell you this with Julie as a witness. Your .3030 won't do more than piss that bear off. It would eventually kill him if you got six or seven shots into his boiler room. It would take an hour, or so, for him to bleed out. Before then, he won't even feel it because of adrenaline. Do yourself a favor. Borrow a .3006 and hope you have someplace to dive after you've emptied it into him. That's the lightest caliber of rifle I'd ever use if I knew I were going to face a grizzly. I killed that other grizz with a .300 magnum. Took three shots from fifteen feet. Does that give you an idea of what this is all about?"

"I thought the police wouldn't shoot at that bear a' tall," Payne said.

"Well, I have to get on the road. Julie, do Jack a favor and tell him what really happened. If it doesn't scare the shit out of him, do him a favor and kick him off your ranch. I don't want to come back here to hunt down another man killing grizzly."

Julie walked with Yellowhenry back to his cruiser. "I want to kiss you so bad, Joe," she said, "but Jack is watching, and he is really jealous."

"Well, let me make this real clear to him and to you," he said. "If you and I are going to be seeing each other, I'm not going to behave to please him." He set his Stetson on the roof of his car. Then, he reached around her waist and bent her over his left thigh and kissed her deeply and passionately. She wrapped her arms around his neck and responded. He kissed her three times before he stood her up. With his hat set back on his head, he took her face in his hands and kissed her again. He looked at Payne and called, "I'll be taking Miss King out from time to time, Jack. Don't make the mistake of trying to interfere." Julie was standing, trembling with one hand on the car. Yellowhenry looked at her and grinned. Just for the hell of it, he dipped her again. "Too much?" he asked as he set her up on her feet.

"I never want it to stop," she whispered.

"If we play our cards right, Julie," he said, "it won't."

What neither of them saw was Julie's mother peaking around a living room curtain giving her husband a blow by blow description of the scene at Yellowhenry's cruiser. "My God, Newt," she breathed delightedly, "he's dipped her down and is kissing her over his knee."

As she reported, he clenched and pumped his fist and repeated again and again, "Yes, yes, yes!"

The snake fence was installed and the inside roundup of the wild ones was conducted. Altogether, fourteen snakes were captured and tossed into the bullpen. James and Charlie decided to contain all of them for a few days to see how many were still loose inside the clinic. A few on the loose would be necessary to control the feral mouse population. All the workers came back and were surprised and gratified to discover how effective the fence was. Charlie walked the perimeter every morning with a capture bucket and a set of tongs. At first he was gathering between five and ten snakes a day. All of them, after being milked, went into the bullpen. Following that, they, along with their captured brothers from the inside roundup, were processed for their meat, skin, and rattles.

Susie had developed a hat banding process in which she trimmed snakeskins and wet sealed the skins to western straw hats. With some, she actually left the heads intact and elevated over the front brims. Hats with seven or more rattles, fetched a premium price, but her price for the head intact hats was more than double that of the simple banded variety. Even with the added price, the demand for the head intact hats was never ending. "Ghoul sells," Minnie told the girl. "Give the gouls what they want, but make 'em pay through the ass for it."

Chapter 46

Fall colors were in full bloom a month later. James was once again a star on the high school rodeo team, but his roping partner was Rope Charles. His girlfriend had spent the summer barrel racing and had fallen for a steer wrestler. Her family had sprung for a horse trailer with a utility apartment in the nose. The wrestler had moved in, including his horse. When she had left the circuit to go back to school, he dumped her and took up with an older barrel racer with the same setup. That Cindy Chattsworth was only seventeen was of little concern to the twenty-two year old steer wrestler. The code was that barrel racers, regardless of age, became a part of the free sex scene that enveloped pro-rodeo. None of the barrel racers thought anything of it. They accepted, enjoyed, and engaged in the expected sex that was just part of the business.

When Cindy approached James to resume their team roping partnership, he politely declined. When she suggested that they could be a couple, he said, "I'd like to date you, Cindy, but I think we're past going steady."

"I get it," she smiled seductively. "Don't make a final decision, though, until I show you what I've learned."

James had turned sixteen that August and his appetite for girls had amped up considerably. He had received his driving permit and Yellowhenry had signed for a used car with the caveat that James help ferry his younger brothers and sisters around when it would be helpful. Even though the contract for the car was in Yellowhenry's name, James was responsible for making the payments. Having a rolling bedroom, made James agreement an automatic. The car was a four year Chevrolet Impala, which was great for hauling siblings and spacious for capers in the dark with his female classmates.

The first dance of the year was a Halloween costume ball that James attended with Cindy. She dressed as a bar room floozy and he left the house looking like any other rodeo cowboy with a big hat and chaps. After picking up Cindy, however, he removed his pants. He was wearing a pair of Cindy's high, French cut black underwear such that his ass cheeks were in evidence through the gap of his chaps.

Since the dance was in a community hall and not at the high school, he went unchallenged. There were many other costumes that were even more risque than his.

Nevertheless, Cindy availed herself of the opportunity to straddle James in slow dances affront while cupping and kneading his ass cheeks. By the time they entered the backseat arena of his Impala, they were both aflame with desire. James received the first installment of his doctorate in sex education from his athletic instructor who had up to then been little more than a throw rug in their prior experience.

Just as he had feared, Yellowhenry found himself sucked in by reputation and experience into another bear hunt. Jack Payne in a jealous rage had decided that the only way to elevate his romantic prospects with Julie was to go out and bag a goddamned grizzly by himself, by God. Twelve hours after he went missing, his hounds, one severely crippled, and his horse with the saddle spun to its belly, returned to the ranch headquarters.

Newton King had Julia pull his .300 magnum from the living room closet and instructed Julie on how to load and handle the big rifle. "Honey," he said, "this is something I should be doing myself."

"Dad, I'll be careful," she assured.

"Now, you listen to me," he said sternly. "Once you find out what happened to that idiot, you come back. Don't go trying to follow that damned bear. It's possible, hell likely, that Payne got himself killed. Look for birds. Use binoculars so you don't get too close. They'll be feeding on the body. Then, watch for any sign of that bear. If he's making a food source out of the body, he'll lay up and take a run at the birds from time to time. If he does, Julie, you get the hell out of there.

"Take the pack mule in case you can bring the body back. Use that big canvas grain bag in the tack room for a body bag. You'll have to smoke out yellowjackets, honey. Sorry to be so graphic, but that's what you'll be dealing with. Take the wasp smoker with you. And take your cell phone so you can get to a high point and let us know what's going on."

Julie struck out for the far back reaches of the ranch into the same terrain that Yellowhenry had been in when he hunted and tracked the first bear. She had ridden the area several times on her pinto, a black and white gelding she called Devil. He was a nine year old with a steady, well-disciplined disposition. Julie felt very safe on his back and she rode confidently to where she decided to drop off the mule so she wouldn't be encumbered with dragging him along.

She had been three hours on the ride, a half hour without the mule and no sign of birds, when she decided to dismount and make water. The sagebrush covered terrain was lightly sprinkled by pine and ash trees and occasional tamaracks leading down to the heavy line of willows that straddled the stream at the base of a long ridge that dominated the entire area.

She was just pulling up her pants when she heard a holler coming from the direction of the willows. At first she looked along the ground. When the call was repeated, she looked up into the branches of a large ash tree some forty yards ahead of where she was zipping up her Wranglers. Payne was perched about twenty-five feet up where he was clinging to the trunk with his legs locked at the ankles around a big branch.

She turned her back to complete her task. "Jack," she yelled. "You could have let me know you were there! You didn't have to spy on me."

"That's all you've ever give me," he shouted. "Not like that cop you just met."

"Get down from there and let's get out of here before I leave you to walk back," she yelled.

Suddenly he began waving and screaming, "Run, Julie! Run! Here comes the bear."

She turned and leaped for the saddle horn as Devil spotted the bear, spun, dropped to his haunches, and began a dirt throwing run back the way he had come. She caught the horn and swung her legs up beside his front quarters where she tapped them to the ground and used the impetus to spring to her saddle. As her hat flew off, she glanced back under her left arm to see the head down, sprinting form of a grizzly bear that was rapidly gaining ground on her and Devil. "Devil!" she squealed, "Run."

The bear had closed enough to take a swipe at the horse just ahead of his nose. His claws scraped hair, hide, and blood in a shallow furrow that made Devil squeal and pour on the coal. With the bear thrown slightly off balance and the increased speed of the horse, the gap between the pair widened until the bear finally pulled up and watched as the racing horse and rider disappeared across a swale.

As Devil pounded up the far side of the shallow depression, Julie looked back and saw that the bear had shut off its pursuit, so she began slowing her horse down until she could finally get him stopped. She jumped off and immediately examined the animal's hind quarters. Her relief was vast when she saw the superficial scratches. She pulled the still frightened horse around to where he could see that he was no longer being pursued. After talking to him soothingly, she reduced his latent panic to where she could remount him without his attempts to turn from under her step to the stirrup and head back to the barn.

She rode to where she could see Payne. He had moved even further up in the tree. She waved her canteen in the air, and dropped it from the top of her hand, hoping he could see that she was leaving him water. Then she rode to where she had tethered the mule. She left Payne to his own devices as she rode home.

Chapter 47

Julie rode her horse into the stable where she unsaddled him and tied the bridle reins to a ring. She packed her gear into the tack room and heaved the saddle onto a saddle horse. Then she pulled a tub of salve from a medicine locker and went to treat Devil's rump.

She had just untied her horse after swabbing on the salve and pulled his bridle so he could walk to a hay manger under an opening in the loft floor, when her parents came into the barn with her mother pushing her father's wheelchair. "Why didn't you call us?" her father demanded.

"I guess I forgot after the bear swatted Devil. Luckily, it's just a scratch."

"Oh, my god," he yowled. "I nearly sent my own daughter to her death."

"No you didn't, Dad. I would have gone out there either way."

"Well, no more without Yellowhenry. That's all there is to it. Where's Jack?"

"Up a tree where he belongs," she said vehemently.

"What do you mean up a tree, Julie?" Julia asked.

"That's what he gets for spyin' on me pissin'," she replied.

"Why was he up there, Julie?"

"I guess he outclimbed the bear. We didn't get to compare notes."

"So he was still alive when you left."

"I left him my canteen so he has water if the bear lets him out of the tree."

"We need to call Yellowhenry and launch a rescue," King said. "Right now."

Russel Thistle took the call. "Something about bears, Captain," he said, handing off the phone.

He watched as Yellowhenry's face paled the longer he listened. "Okay, I'll be out in a couple of hours. Call the Phillips County Sheriff's Office. The sheriff's office takes the lead in these cases, Newt. No, I can't get there in time to go out today, and we will not go out there in the dark. Just hold pat until I get there. Okay, good. Make sure Julie waits, too."

"Sounds serious," Thistle commented.

"Hard to tell at this point, Russ, but I have to go out to a ranch out east of here. I could be gone for two or three days. Get James and Minnie to help out. I'll be taking Hi Boy. Double check with the office in the morning and tell Art to take over. I'll call in sometime tomorrow."

"Hell of a way to spend Sunday afternoon, Captain."

"Comes with the territory. I need my emergency pack of food and water and my bedroll. If you can set those out, I'll get my gun and go load my horse."

Yellowhenry had upgraded his rifle after the bear hunt that had resulted in Trooper Zane Hammond's near death experience. He had scored on a used Remington lever action .300 Magnum. While he could have requisitioned one through the highway patrol, he didn't because he wanted his own personalized weapon, one he could carry in a saddle scabbard and trust it would hit where he aimed it. He left for the King ranch a half hour later.

When he pulled into the ranch yard, Sheriff Al Sparks was already in the house drinking coffee and putting moves on Julie. "Well, Captain Grizzly Killer, we meet for another bear hunt," Sparks said jovially, rising to shake hands.

Yellowhenry chuckled, "Hello, Al. Are you ready for another swim in a beaver pond?"

Sparks laughed nervously, "Well, no. I was just telling the Kings, here, about that last one. I guess I forgot about the beaver pond."

"That's all right, Al. I was here the other day and told them all about it."

"Julie's already been out there on this one. Bear ran her back. Nicked her horse's ass," Sparks advised.

"Is that so?" Yellowhenry queried. "What did I say about going after grizzlies, Julie?"

"I don't remember exactly," she blushed.

"I do. One, don't go alone. Two, don't go with inexperienced people. You broke all that in one ride," he smiled. "Do you believe me, now?"

"I was going to rescue Jack. Someone had to do it," she said haughtily. "I wasn't going after a bear."

"That's the problem with grizzlies; they can't tell when you are and when you aren't after them. To a Griz, it's all the same. They're also convinced they own the country. Top of the food chain mentality."

"Well, I'm sorry, Captain Yellowhenry, that I didn't get a permission slip from you. Al, would you care for a refill? I'll be happy to get it," she smiled sweetly. Then sourly, "Oh, would you care for coffee, Captain Yellowhenry."

"I'll pass, thanks," he said abruptly. "Newt, if you don't mind, I'll put my horse in a stable. I'll throw my bedroll in the bunkhouse. I'd like to borrow your mule tomorrow, if that's all right. I'll be heading out at daylight in the morning."

"Yeah, sure," King said. "Pack saddle's in the tack room. Big grain bag in there if you need it."

"Thanks, I have my own pack saddle with the stuff I need."

"I'll ride with you, Captain," Julie said, coming back from the kitchen with the coffee pot.

"Well, that's Sheriff Spark's job, but he doesn't ride out after grizzly bears anymore, do you, Al?" Yellowhenry chuckled.

"No, I don't. End of report," Sparks laughed loudly. "I'll run ground central, but I ain't goin' out in the rough and ready."

"So, I'll be on my own tomorrow then, Julie," Yellowhenry said as he turned to leave the ranch house. "Al will be needing you here to pour his coffee."

Chapter 48

Not wanting to be sandbagged by Julie rising early and attempting to join him despite their conversation of the previous evening, Yellowhenry left before dawn. When she knocked on the bunkhouse door at daybreak with her apology rehearsed, and he didn't appear, her heart sank. Then she strode to the barn and saddled Devil, anyway.

Yellowhenry rode in half circles taking his time. When daylight came he was on a high point searching with binoculars for the ash tree Payne was sitting in when Julie left him by himself. He was pretty sure he had spotted it, when he saw Julie riding straight for it. "Well, hell, here we go," he muttered. He dismounted Hi Boy and tethered the mule. Then he remounted and rode to cross Julie's line of approach.

When he was a couple of hundred yards short of crossing her tracks, he spotted several magpies in a flock on the ground. He immediately jumped from Hi Boy, ground tied him, pulled his rifle from the saddle scabbard, and sprinted down the shoulder of a low hill in front of him. When he felt he was far enough from Hi Boy that a shot wouldn't spook him, he slid to his butt and jacked a round into his rifle and fired into the air. The boom of the shot caused Julie to jerk Devil around to face the direction of the shot.

When she saw Yellowhenry standing and waving his hat, she started to ride toward him until he dropped his hat and waved her away with his hand. At first she began trotting off so she could look back at what was happening. Then she saw Yellowhenry taking a rest with his rifle propped between his knees. He seemed to be waiting for something. When she saw the brown blur streaking toward her, she instantly began whipping Devil into a run.

The distance between the bear and the horse was only fifteen yards and closing when Yellowhenry's shot creased the bear's back just behind its hump. It was a flesh wound but the impact was enough to tip him over. When he regained his feet, the bear was off toward the willows at the base of the ridge. Yellowhenry fired another round, but the big bruin had turned to avoid a boulder and the shot went wide. The bear went out of sight in a shallow draw that led into the willows.

Yellowhenry ignored Julie as she raced into the distance. Wearily, he turned and climbed back up the hill to where he'd left Hi Boy. He mounted up and rode to where the mule stood where he'd been tethered. Grim faced, Yellowhenry headed for where he'd seen the magpies. They flew off, cackling, as he approached what they had been feeding on. It was what he'd expected.

It was clear that Jack Payne had decided to take his chances. He had waited till dark, expecting that the bear would leave the area, but it hadn't. Less than two hundred yards from the big ash, the bear had caught a running Payne from behind. Death had, at least, been swift.

Yellowhenry began the process of recovering the remains. Most of the torso along with the arms and head were still intact. The internal organs and legs were nearly totally consumed. Yellowhenry, feeling guilty, gave thanks that yellowjackets hadn't yet swarmed the cavity of the ribs or the gaping mouth. He had just spread the body bag out beside the body when he saw Julie riding his way.

In a moment of ghoulishness, he waited till she reached him. As soon as she saw what was left of Payne, she bailed off Devil and began vomiting off to the side. Yellowhenry waited until she stood up. "All done?" he asked.

"What?" she asked, "Why would you ask me that?"

"Because, Julie, you wanted to get involved in this. Insisted on it. Well, here it is. It isn't pretty. And that bear is still out there. He was guarding his kill when you rode right in on him. I hit him, but from the way he was running, he'll recover. What he does next as it relates to your ranch, is anyone's guess. I hope he leaves. Maybe goes off into Canada somewhere and dies of old age. I sure as hell have had my fill of him. Maybe, now, you have, too. Maybe you have, too," he tiredly repeated.

While he had thought of it, he didn't ask if she wanted to help bag Jack Payne's remains. He figured he had rubbed her nose in it enough. With the bag stowed on the pack saddle of the mule and tied down, Yellowhenry mounted Hi Boy and began riding for the ranch house. He rode silently and without regard to Julie who followed. Twice, she stopped to pick up her canteen and the hat she'd lost the day before. She came loping up to ride beside him. "Joe?" she asked, "Can we talk?"

"What do you want to talk about?" he asked glancing at her.

"I want to apologize for the way I acted yesterday."

"Apology accepted," he said.

"I got the feeling that you don't want to see me."

"You made it plain enough that, at least yesterday, that's what you wanted. Al Sparks is a nice fella, and he can't wait to take my place, Julie. For you it's a win/win. We don't need to talk it out so we both feel better. It just is what it is."

"But I really want to see you, Joe," she pleaded.

He pulled up Hi Boy and leaned forward with crossed arms on his saddle horn. "Let's wait for a while. Right now, I have a lot on my plate to finish with Jack Payne. I really don't know where this will shake out with me and you, Julie. Even that bear is an issue. But this isn't the time to get into it. Romance is the furthest thing from my mind right now."

"Well, at least you know my door is open," she said. "I'll see you back at the ranch." She rode off ahead on her own. Yellowhenry let her go and checked off Julie King's open door as pending.

When Yellowhenry rode into the ranch yard, Phillips County Sheriff Al Sparks was already primed to milk another political opportunity. He had called his office and reported what Julie knew about the bear and the body recovery. The Phillips County coroner had been notified, and the Phillips County News was sending out a reporter and photographer.

U.S. Fish and Wildlife in Malta caught the notice of a mankiller bear on the wide band scanner that covered the various law enforcement agencies in the state. They immediately dispatched an officer to the King Ranch. In addition, citizens of the area picked up the news and spread it like wildfire.

By the time Yellowhenry had unloaded the mule and unsaddled Hi Boy, the congregation was building. The Kings were being interviewed by the news reporter.

When he walked past leading Hi Boy, Yellowhenry was intercepted by the photographer, who recognized him. "Hey, Trooper Joe, I have to get a picture of you and your horse. Those white claw marks on his ass are beautiful."

"Hello, Curt," Yellowhenry said. "Sure, why not?"

With Hi Boy angled a bit and Yellowhenry standing at his head holding his halter rope, the photographer, Curt Bevins, took several shots as he moved in a semicircle, making sure that the marks were featured. Hi Boy had been attacked by the first man killing bear and the deep claw marks to both sides of his rump had healed with the hair growing back in white. The marks had made the horse a celebrity in the area, especially in small town parades.

As Yellowhenry was loading his horse into his trailer, Julie joined him. "What's up?" he asked.

"Are you still mad at me?" she asked.

"Never have been mad at you, Julie. Just put off is all."

"Those are claw marks on your horse, huh?" she asked.

"Courtesy of this ranch," Yellowhenry said. He tugged Hi Boy into the trailer and tied him off.

"Well, they certainly are distinctive scars."

"Yeah, this horse and I have both collected scars from this place," he said.

Chapter 49

When Yellowhenry had finished with all the reports and interviews, the rancher, Newt King, asked for a private word with him. His wife and daughter were entertaining Sheriff Sparks and Slim Cranston of the U.S. Fish and Wildlife Service in the kitchen while the two were talking quietly in the living room. "This is kind of hard for me, Joe," King began. "But I need to give you a bit of history. My daughter married the wrong man. She may have told you that she couldn't produce any children. Well, that's not true. She conceived three times and he caused her to miscarry all three times. He was a violent prick, Joe. Beat her without leaving visible marks. Body blows. She blamed herself, though, because she wanted to make the marriage stick. Lucky for her, he fell out of a boat on a duck hunt. He was alone and drowned before he could be rescued. He was a lawman, too."

"He sure as hell didn't set a very good example for a lawman," Yellowhenry offered.

"I take it you don't cotton to men beating women," King said.

"They're the worst kind. Whenever I get one on staff in my office, I get rid of him as soon as possible."

"Good on you, Joe," King said. "Julie is still hung up on her ex because ever since she was a little girl, she has wanted to be around lawmen and women. Part of your attraction for her was your car and uniform. Her mother and I were delighted when you were so physically drawn to each other. We spied on you, Captain Yellowhenry."

"We had it going for a moment, there," Yellowhenry grinned.

"Julia and I want it to continue."

"That's pretty much up to Julie, isn't it?"

"And you, Captain. Please don't shut her out. We fear she's wasting into spinsterism."

"Well, Sheriff Sparks is showing a rather keen interest in her. He's a lawman."

"And proud of hiding under the kitchen table when the heavy lifting starts. Like going after that bear."

"Well, Newt, if you had had to swim into beaver lodges to keep from being killed by a grizzly, you might understand where his being leery comes from."

"If close calls count, you're the one who really has the experience."

"Not much of a recommendation, Newt."

"To Julie, it's everything. It's pure and brave and responsible. Julie has her cap set for you, Trooper Joe. I pray to God, for her sake, that you don't take her feelings lightly. She's more fragile than she knows."

"I'm glad we had this talk, Newt. I will take care."

When he walked into the patrol offices the next morning, Yellowhenry was looking forward to clearing his desk and having a cup of coffee while he read the newspaper. What he saw was his picture with Hi Boy under a headline that read: YELLOWHENRY WOUNDS ANOTHER MANKILLER. The story was written from AP reports by Willie Little who dredged up old history about bear attacks and made condescending statements about how the local state patrol captain could benefit from firing range practice time that was required of the troopers under his command. An undisclosed highway patrol source was quoted as saying that while the captain maintained the standard for handguns, he was rarely, if ever, observed on the rifle range. Perhaps he could shoot straighter if he practiced more. And so on, and so on.

Yellowhenry had swung his legs down from his desk and was gritting his teeth as he did a slow burn while he reread the article.

"Well, that Willie Tiny Dick can really spin a yarn, eh, Barbara?" Art McClintock said from the door to Yellowhenry's private office where they had slipped quietly to observe their captain's reaction to the story.

"Oh, yeah. Master storyteller," Barbara Premminger said seriously. "Masterful writer. Masterful."

"Very funny, you two," Yellowhenry growled. "Very funny. But when that dickhead comes here today for comment from me for his follow up story tomorrow, tell him I'm unavailable. That asshole! Rifle range practice? There's no MHP requirement for rifle range practice. And that's another thing. Who the hell told that hack that I don't practice on the rifle range. Do you know who would have said that?"

"Not offhand," Art said. "We could call everyone in, though. Third degree 'em."

"Maybe if Trooper Joe offered a reward for whoever comes clean, the scoundrel could be rounded up and made to spill his guts," Barbara added hopefully, looking seriously at McClintock.

"Yeah, great idea. Joe, how much can we offer?"

"Ha, ha, ho, ho. A thousand dollars. For Chrissakes, I don't get no respect around here," Yellowhenry grumbled.

"I did it!" Barbara and Art shouted simultaneously.

Just then Yellowhenry's phone rang and he picked up. "Yellowhenry," he said sternly. "Oh, it's you Mr. Little. No, I do not care to comment." He slammed the receiver viciously back into its cradle. "And fuck you!" he shouted leaning down for emphasis.

"Well, maybe we oughta go back to our duties, Barbara," Art said as he eased out of the doorway.

"Yeah, I think we oughta," she said with a sideways grin. "Good talk, Captain. Let's do it again real soon."

Yellowhenry fumed for the rest of the morning. When lunchtime came, he decided to have a sandwich at the Cascade Mountains Restaurant. The place was so packed he had to wait for a table or booth, and he was just about to forget it and leave when he saw someone waving frantically from the far side of the restaurant to catch his attention. Rather than wave back, he decided to walk over to where the person was to say a friendly hello. Halfway there he recognized Julia King. She and her husband were sitting on one side of a booth and Julie was seated with her back to him on the opposite side of her parents.

Newt's wheelchair was folded up and leaned against the divider between booths. "Please join us, Captain," Julia smiled. "You'll never get a spot if you don't."

"Well, thank you," he said. "You're definitely right about that." He hung his Stetson on the rack attached to the divider and slid in next to Julie. "What brings you folks to town today?" he asked.

"Couple of things," Newt answered. "I have therapy for my back once a week, even though it seems like a waste of time. And we're looking for a ranch hand to replace Payne. Have to set up services for Jack, too. His family wants him buried here. They're having a private memorial for him in South Dakota. That's where he's from. Hell, there wasn't enough left of him to embalm. We're paying for the burial next weekend. You're invited to attend. It's just a graveside service."

"I'll do that if I can," Yellowhenry said. "What a sad end to life."

Chapter 50

The lunch with the Kings was very pleasant. Yellowhenry and Julie became quite friendly. She invited him out to the ranch for a horseback ride, and for some reason out of the blue, he made it a date. King was concerned that the bear would return and asked Yellowhenry if he had any ideas on how to ambush him. "Get some chickens," Yellowhenry advised. "A wounded bear will be looking for easy prey. Chickens are that, and they set up a hell of a racket that will give you warning. Shoot from that second story bedroom window overlooking the chicken coop. It's only a seventy-five yard shot. Julie, that'd be your job. There's a yard light out there, and the switch is in the kitchen. Keep that light turned off until you hear the chickens. When Julie is in position, Julia you'll flip that light on. Shoot straight, Julie. Oh, yeah. Get yourself a set of muffs for ear protection. That .300 of your dad's will blow your eardrums out when you shoot inside the house if you don't plug your ears."

"I told you we needed chickens," Julia scolded her husband.

"Yeah, but not as bear bait," Newt said. "Julie, you'll have to take care of them."

"I can do that. But where do we get chickens?"

"Joe, do you know?"

"Well, most people around here order them online as chicks. The bus brings them in as far as I know. You might have to go to neighbors and buy them."

"I guess so," Newt said. "Damned chickens. Dirtiest bird on the planet."

"After you kill the bear, turn 'em loose," Yellowhenry suggested. "As a free range bird, they care for themselves. If you get Bantams, they even learn to fly when the coyotes and foxes get after 'em."

"Won't the coyotes and foxes wipe them out?" Julie asked.

"Oh, eventually. Hawks and weasels and bobcats along with your barn cats will help, too," Yellowhenry said helpfully.

"I like that," Newt said.

"We're not doing that," Julia said firmly. "I want some layers for eggs. And some fryers, while we're talking about it."

"Help me out, Joe," Newt laughed.

"Hire a chicken plucker as your hired man," Yellowhenry grinned.

Chapter 51

The date ride with Julie King took place three weeks later. When Yellowhenry pulled into the ranch yard, he noticed that the chicken coop was loaded with a flock of Rhode Island Reds. Julie met him at the kitchen door and wrapped him in a welcoming kiss and embrace.

"Whoa," he exclaimed, "let me step back and come in again."

"Go ahead," she laughed. "Let's do it all day. Come on in, Joe. Let me fetch you a cup of coffee. Daddy has something he wants to talk to you about."

After greeting the Kings, Yellowhenry asked, "How goes the bear hunting, Newt?"

"So far, a bobcat, two black bears, and a cougar."

"I take it Julie shoots pretty good," Yellowhenry chuckled.

"Yeah, she does now. To start with, she missed a wolf, a fox, and three coyotes."

"That's quite an impressive list of predators," Yellowhenry said. "When did you make your last kill, Julie?"

"Three nights ago. But the chickens have stopped making much of a fuss. They're getting used to prowlers, I guess."

"Well, there you go," he said. "A grizzly won't be stopped by that fence, though. What did you do with those critters you shot?"

"The hired man took care of the carcasses. The hides are nailed to the back wall of the barn."

"Those black bears and the cougar need to be reported to Fish and Game if you haven't already," Yellowhenry advised.

"All taken care of," King said. "My new hired man knew we needed to file a report."

"So, you've hired a new hand already?" Yellowhenry asked.

"Jose Escheveria. Comes from the Basque country of Spain. He's a citizen now, though. Spent the last ten years on ranches down Colorado way. So far, he's been damned good with the chores," King said.

"I see," Yellowhenry smiled. "And he took care of the remains, you say."

"Yessir," King said, "gutted and skinned and whatever else. Used the mule to dump the rest into a gulley out east a half mile, or so. He was eager to do it, and Julie had no interest in it at all. Worked out beautifully."

"Julie said there was something you wanted to discuss, Newt."

"Yeah, about Jose. He seems off a bit. Doesn't always react naturally to being called 'Jose.' It's like he's using an assumed name. He eats down in the bunkhouse even after we told him he could eat his meals with us. And he has a habit of ducking out of sight whenever anyone comes around. He also took a half day off to run into Havre after Julie shot the bears. That seemed odd. I thought maybe you should know about all that. What do you think?"

"Did he explain why after ten years on ranches in Colorado he suddenly shows up here?"

"Not really. He said he just wanted to see the country."

"He has no family, I take it?"

"All in Spain."

"Hold on a minute while I run out to my pickup," Yellowhenry said. When he returned he was carrying a three ring binder that was two-thirds full of Wanted Posters. He leafed through it until he found the flyer on a man named Gerardia Torres. He removed it from the binder and handed it to King. "Is this your hired man?" Yellowhenry asked.

"Well, I'll be damned," King cursed. "Sure as hell. What's he wanted for?"

"Read the flyer, Newt. It's all there."

King took his time and finally, frowning, looked up. "I don't see a lot here that would scare a man into hiding out from everyone. Way back he was involved in drugs. User, I'd guess. Marijuana use it looks like. That's legal in a lot of states nowadays. Failure to appear in court. Jumped bail on a recognizance bond. No violence, theft, burglary, or assault and battery. Quite frankly, it's all petty stuff."

"Look down there toward the bottom." Yellowhenry said. "Do you see something that ties into what he's been doing here on your ranch?"

"Oh, there it is. He's been named in a black market ring dealing in animal parts."

"Bear gall bladders, primarily, but other organs, as well. It raises the stakes, these days. I'm sorry, but I have to arrest him, Newt. His claim to be a citizen might well be bogus, too. When Immigration and Naturalization agents show up anywhere these days, you'd be surprised at the people hightailing it."

"Well, hell. Back to the drawing board. Damnit. This Torres, amongst his nefarious feats, has developed into a very good ranch hand. What a waste. Well, he'll be down at the barn, Joe."

"You mean, now?" Julie asked. "Joe and I are going horseback riding."

"Sorry, Julie," Yellowhenry said. "I have a duty that comes first."

He retrieved his hat and walked out to his rig where he pulled on his service belt before walking to the barn. Julie watched anxiously through the window of the kitchen door. Yellowhenry unsnapped the flap on his holster, drew the weapon, and pushed the barn door open. He stood to the side of the door frame for a moment before sticking his head into the door and looking around.

When he disappeared inside, Julie's anxiety overcame her and she hurried across the yard to peek around the edge of the barn door. Yellowhenry saw her shadow and sneaked along beside the horse stalls. She moved inside, keeping the door in front of her as a shield. Suddenly, as she prepared to sneak a look around the door's edge, a hand snaked around and grabbed her left forearm. She was jerked inside where she stumbled and fell to the floor. When she looked up, Yellowhenry stood dumbfounded above her. "Julie!" he yelled. "I could have shot you. What the hell are you doing?"

"I was afraid for you," she said, her lip trembling.

"All right. Okay," he said, putting his sidearm back into its holster, "no harm, no foul." He reached a hand down to help her up. She rose nimbly and smoothly into his willing embrace. They kissed with hunger and need. Thoughts of his session with Carolyn Malone in one of the stalls just behind him flooded his brain, and he very nearly led Julie for a return visit. Instead, he pulled away from her and said, "Sweetheart, let's save this for later. Torres is gone and so is Devil."

Chapter 52

Julie was beside herself. "Daddy, that son of a bitch stole my horse! I want him shot," she raged.

"Of course," he couldn't help but laugh. "We'll shoot him at sunrise tomorrow. Can you stay overnight and do the honors, Trooper Joe?"

"Well, I have an idea that involves my staying overnight. Maybe we'll just arrest Torres."

"Do you think he's just gonna turn around and come back?" Julie asked.

"Yes, as long as he figures that I have gone. So, I'm going to drive down to that wide spot a couple of miles down toward the highway and stash my pickup and trailer there. I'll ride Hi Boy back and stall him so he's out of sight. Then we'll wait for Torres to reappear."

"Do you think he'll stay out all night," Newt asked.

"Julie, do you object to riding double?"

"Well, I can. Do you mean behind you?"

"Yes. I thought we'd ride out in a circle and scout the country for that Griz. We'll be back this afternoon kinda late. Have dinner and along toward dark, I'll pull out. Torres is likely to come back in before morning if he thinks I'm gone, and I'll be waiting in the bunkhouse for him."

"Let me pack a lunch for you, Julia said. You two are bound to get hungry if you're going to be out that late."

With Julie mounted behind him, Yellowhenry rode Hi Boy out on the rough ranch road that wound through the scrub and rock outcrops toward the big ridge that dominated the skyline to the north and west of the ranch property. The weather was warm and sunny. It was a good day for a ride. Julie was able to put fears for her horse away. She rode, at first, holding onto the saddle strings adjacent to both sides of the cantle. Yellowhenry stopped from time to time and looked over the country with binoculars. A couple of hours into the ride, he stopped for a piss break.

When they mounted up to resume, Julie pulled her denim jacket off and spread it out on Hi Boy's rump and the back of the saddle. She was wearing a gray long sleeved snapped button cotton shirt. Beneath the shirt, she wore nothing. When they resumed riding, she sat on the coat but didn't ride holding the saddle strings. Instead she used her hands on Yellowhenry's back to maintain her balance. He had also removed his jacket and tucked it behind the pommel in front of his waist. Shortly, he decided to ride to a high point to look around. As Hi Boy pulled upward into the slope, Julie leaned forward, wrapped her arms around him, and flattened her breasts against his back.

At the top they dismounted, kissed fervently, and laid the jackets out on the ground. The next time they stopped was for lunch. They spread the jackets out again after they ate. Afterward they stretched out in the grass and talked about what their possibilities were. "Julie, I have seven kids. I know that you are aware of that, but are you sure you could cope in a household like that?"

"I think we'll know more after we've been engaged for a while."

"Let's just date until we are sure we can stand each other when sex is not in the offing."

"Are you getting cold feet already?"

"Already? Julie, this is our first date."

"I know," she said, "but it isn't our first rodeo."

"That's even more reason to be sensible," he said. "With time, we're expected to make wise and sure decisions."

"I'm sure right now," she said. "Trust me. I'm ready to jump off the deep end."

He laughed, rolled over, and kissed her. "Go ahead, I'll wade from the shallow end, if you don't mind."

She giggled, "I can see I have a lot more sex to endure. My turn on top." She rolled him to his back onto a litter of small volcanic stones. He didn't feel them at all.

When they rode in at dusk, Yellowhenry tended to Hi Boy. Then he slapped Julie on the rump, "Do you know what you smell like?"

"Raw sex." she squealed. "Never better."

"Yeah, maybe," he laughed, "but I'm not sitting at the dinner table with your folks while their eyes are watering. Come on. We're gonna take a quick shower in the bunkhouse before we walk up to the house."

"Oh, my god," she said. "More sex. It's a tough job, but some girl's gotta do it."

The next morning an hour before daylight Yellowhenry was sitting fully dressed on a bunk along the back wall of the bunkhouse. He heard a horse walk past to the barn. Fifteen minutes later, he greeted Gerardia Torres, "Sir, you are under arrest," he said.

Torres tried to dart back out the door, but Yellowhenry had anticipated that and shouldered the door closed. Torres took a wild swing that missed at the same time that Yellowhenry swung at him. Yellowhenry's blow, aided by his pistol, struck Torres along the left jaw and temple, knocking him out.

"Did you get him?" Julie called from the back wall.

"He's down," Yellowhenry replied.

"Good. Cuff him to a leg of the kitchen range," she said. "And

come back to bed. You're needed."

Chapter 53

As the year wound down to the holidays, Yellowhenry was beset by problems that put a damper on his budding romance with Julie. Three of his officers transferred to other jurisdictions, leaving the Havre sector shorthanded for over a month. As a result, Yellowhenry took up patrol duties from time to time to cut down on the overtime expense to his budget. He saw Julie twice in a month and a half.

Charlie Goodwoman and Minnie Graves had announced their engagement. But the more she thought about it, the less she liked the idea. Charlie refused to live anywhere but at the apartment at the serpentarium. While spending a night there, she retired to the bathroom in the middle of the night to find a wild one crawling and rattling its way into a corner where it rose into a striking pose. After that she attended only during daylight hours while wearing snake proof boots.

Both of them appealed to Yellowhenry for a solution to the dilemma. His advice was for them to buy a decent vehicle so Charlie could sleep at Minnie's and drive both of them to the serpentarium to work during the day. When Minnie objected to being stuck there all day, Yellowhenry exploded. "How damned much money do you have stockpiled right now, Minnie?"

"I'm not exactly sure. Around two hundred thousand, though."

"Then buy two cars," an exasperated Yellowhenry exclaimed.

Russel Thistle had given thirty day notice that he had taken a job in Arizona. "I have enjoyed my time with your family, Joe, but ask any of the women I've known. I have sand in my shoes. I can't help it and I want to spend the winter where it's warm."

Yellowhenry had dropped his head and begun chuckling. When Thistle asked if he'd said something funny, he said, "No. Russ. Nothing funny, just a comment from a page out of my own book. I'll let you go on one condition."

"What's that?" Thistle asked.

"That you replace yourself first."

"But of course," Thistle smiled. "A miss Lydia Amato will be training in from Grand Junction, Colorado next week."

"Really? Who is she?" Yellowhenry asked.

"She is very highly recommended and has had formal training in childcare. I know because she is my own twenty-eight year old daughter."

The one good spot of news was that Newt King had leased his ranch out to a hunting club, specializing in deer hunting. The grizzly that had been wounded by Yellowhenry had recovered from the flesh wound, but instead of raiding at the ranch headquarters it feasted on gut piles and killed deer carcasses hung up by the hunters of the hunting club for later retrieval. As a result, the great bear had fed its hyperphagia well enough that it denned up early when a series of blizzards swept out of Canada bringing in a long, cold, and deadly winter.

The End